The Book of Aran

Visual Guide

Text & Illustrations

Michael Rocha

Published by Aeon Publishing, a division of Axis Mundi, Inc.

Aeon Publishing
539 Allensville Rd
Sevierville Tennessee 37876
office.aeonpublishing@gmail.com

ISBN 979-8-218-57826-8

MIDDLEVERSE

Table of Content

The House of Aran
Guardians of the Desert Realms

Introduction

The House of Aran, a storied and proud civilization, traces its origins to an ancient offshoot of the House of Abraxas. Over the centuries, the Aran have thrived on the desert planet Zarah, one of six planets in the Leander System. Though the other planets are home to different Houses, the Aran live mostly in isolation, unaware of their many cosmic neighbours, focused entirely on the vast desert expanses of their own world. Zarah is a land of harsh extremes, where various types of deserts, from arid and cold plains to scorching dunes, shape the people's culture, governance, and daily life. Unlike other desert dwellers from distant star systems, such as the Gurun, who live in mixed desert and woodland environments, the Aran are a people defined entirely by their intimate relationship with the deserts, both cold and hot, and their ability to flourish within them. Their culture is centred on their mastery of desert survival, horse breeding, intricate artistic traditions, and a deep-seated warrior ethos. However, beneath their visible grandeur lies a quieter battle against the insidious influence of the House of Draco, whose subtle manipulation threatens to destabilize their society from within.

Zarah

From the scorching dunes of the equatorial regions to the frigid deserts of the northern and southern poles, shaped the Aran in ways unlike any other people in any other system, for hundreds of lightyears in any direction. While other Houses, such as the House of Gurun on a distant star system, found balance between desert and woodland environments, the Aran exist in a singular relationship with their arid world. The House of Aran is not merely a civilization that survives in the desert—they thrive in it, drawing their identity, culture, and way of life from the vast sea of sand and rock that defines Zarah.

Unaware of the existence of occupants on neighbourin planets, the Aran have focused entirely on mastering their own world. Their culture is deeply tied to the desert, not only in a practical sense but also spiritually, artistically, and militarily. The deserts of Zarah are not barren to the Aran; they are alive with potential, full of challenges to overcome, and secrets to unlock. The Aran see themselves as custodians of these vast lands, blessed and burdened with the responsibility of preserving the delicate balance of life and death in a world where the line between the two is often razor-thin.

The Planet of Endless Deserts

Zarah is the third planet from the central star of the Leander System, but unlike many arid planets, Zarah's deserts are not monolithic in nature. Instead, they are varied and complex, each offering unique challenges and resources that the Aran have spent centuries mastering. These deserts fall into five primary types, each forming the basis for each of the six major kingdoms on the planet

Hot Sand Deserts

These vast, undulating dunes dominate the equatorial regions of Zarah. The daytime heat is so intense that the sand can burn your skin, while nights bring cold temperatures. In certain areas, sandstorms, sometimes lasting for days, can reshape entire landscapes overnight, sometimes uncovering ancient ruins long lost to the sands.

Cold Deserts

In the northern and southern polar regions, temperatures drop to very low, and the deserts here are composed of arid plains and rocky tundra. Though snow is rare, the icy winds and reflective expanses of crystalline sand present their own unique dangers

Rocky Deserts

These regions, primarily located in the central highlands, are defined by jagged cliffs, vast stone plateaus, and deep canyons with vast plains. Water exists in the form of rivers, and these areas have long oases, extending for miles. Plants and wildlife have adapted to survive here. The rocky deserts are home to many fortresses and military outposts, built on top of mesas and in the plains situated beneath them

Subtropical Deserts

These deserts experience seasonal rainfalls, which are enough to create life. Oasis towns dot these regions, where the waters are carefully guarded and fiercely fought over.

13

Coastal Deserts

These regions, situated along the planet's bodies of water, are covered in fine sands that stretch to the ocean. The seas of Zarah are deep, filled with dangerous creatures, and their shores are sometimes battered by salt-laden winds.

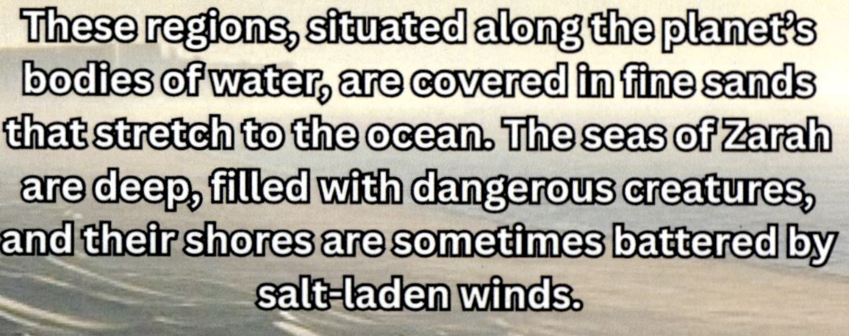

The deserts of Zarah are not just physical features but play a vital role in the spiritual and cultural life of the Aran people. The desert is a teacher, a challenge, and a sacred space. Life in the desert requires constant vigilance, innovation, and respect for nature's power, which has moulded the Aran into a people of both resilience and grace

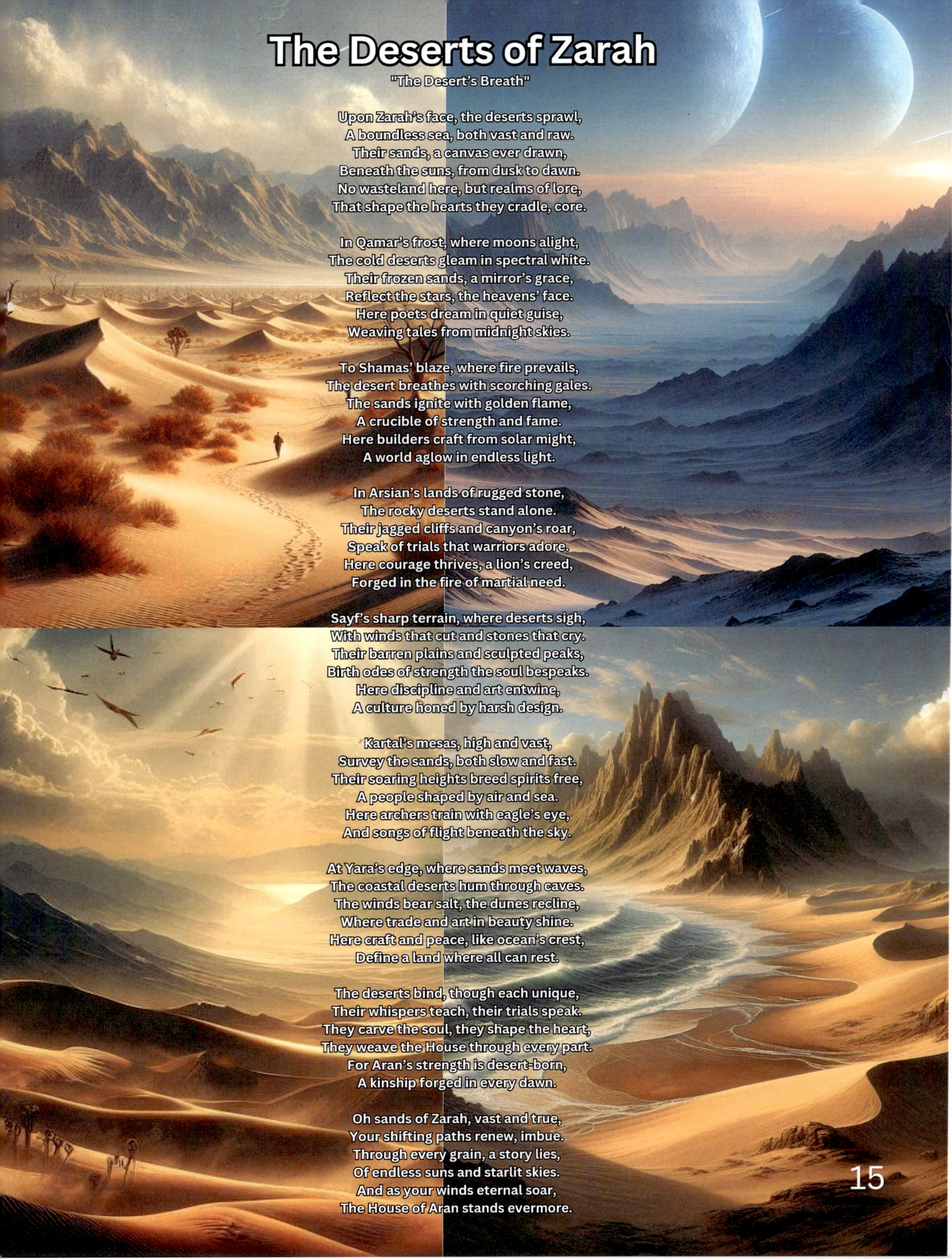

The Deserts of Zarah

"The Desert's Breath"

Upon Zarah's face, the deserts sprawl,
A boundless sea, both vast and raw.
Their sands, a canvas ever drawn,
Beneath the suns, from dusk to dawn.
No wasteland here, but realms of lore,
That shape the hearts they cradle, core.

In Qamar's frost, where moons alight,
The cold deserts gleam in spectral white.
Their frozen sands, a mirror's grace,
Reflect the stars, the heavens' face.
Here poets dream in quiet guise,
Weaving tales from midnight skies.

To Shamas' blaze, where fire prevails,
The desert breathes with scorching gales.
The sands ignite with golden flame,
A crucible of strength and fame.
Here builders craft from solar might,
A world aglow in endless light.

In Arsian's lands of rugged stone,
The rocky deserts stand alone.
Their jagged cliffs and canyon's roar,
Speak of trials that warriors adore.
Here courage thrives, a lion's creed,
Forged in the fire of martial need.

Sayf's sharp terrain, where deserts sigh,
With winds that cut and stones that cry.
Their barren plains and sculpted peaks,
Birth odes of strength the soul bespeaks.
Here discipline and art entwine,
A culture honed by harsh design.

Kartal's mesas, high and vast,
Survey the sands, both slow and fast.
Their soaring heights breed spirits free,
A people shaped by air and sea.
Here archers train with eagle's eye,
And songs of flight beneath the sky.

At Yara's edge, where sands meet waves,
The coastal deserts hum through caves.
The winds bear salt, the dunes recline,
Where trade and art in beauty shine.
Here craft and peace, like ocean's crest,
Define a land where all can rest.

The deserts bind, though each unique,
Their whispers teach, their trials speak.
They carve the soul, they shape the heart,
They weave the House through every part.
For Aran's strength is desert-born,
A kinship forged in every dawn.

Oh sands of Zarah, vast and true,
Your shifting paths renew, imbue.
Through every grain, a story lies,
Of endless suns and starlit skies.
And as your winds eternal soar,
The House of Aran stands evermore.

The Flora of Zarah

The desert planet of Zarah is home to a diverse array of flora that have adapted to thrive in the harsh, arid environment. From the towering desert trees that provide the raw materials for Aran crafts to the resilient shrubs and grasses that dot the sweeping landscapes, the vegetation of Zarah is an integral part of the delicate ecosystem that sustains the House of Aran.

Desert Trees of Zarah

Prominent among the desert trees of Zarah is the majestic Solarwood, a tall, slender tree with a distinctive reddish-brown bark that is highly prized by the Aran people. Solarwood is renowned for its exceptional hardness and durability, making it an ideal material for the construction of musical instruments, furniture, and even the intricate architectural elements that adorn Aran's grand structures.

Desert Trees of Zarah

Another iconic tree of the Aran desert is the Moonleaf, a towering, silver-trunked tree that is revered for its spiritual significance. The Moonleaf's broad, pale green leaves are believed to capture the essence of the twin moons that grace the Aran's night skies, and the tree's wood is often used in the crafting of ceremonial objects and sacred texts.

Desert Trees of Zarah

The Dune Ash, with its twisted, gnarled trunk and delicate, feathery foliage, is a hardy desert tree that thrives in the most arid and inhospitable regions of Zarah. The Aran prize the Dune Ash for its resilience and use its wood to fashion the sturdy frames of their desert dwellings, as well as the sturdy handles of their tools and weapons.

Resilient Desert Shrubs and Grasses

Alongside the towering desert trees, the flora of Zarah is dotted with an eclectic array of hardy shrubs and grasses that have adapted to the harsh, arid conditions. The Sunbloom, a low-growing succulent with vibrant orange flowers, is a common sight across the Aran's desert landscapes, its water-storing leaves, and thick, leathery stems enabling it to survive the most extreme droughts.

Resilient Desert Shrubs and Grasses

The Lunaris, a delicate, white-blossomed shrub that blooms only under the light of the twin moons, is highly prized by the Aran for its medicinal properties, with the plant's leaves and petals being used to create a variety of tinctures and poultices.

Resilient Desert Shrubs and Grasses

The Sand Whisper, a resilient grass with tall, slender stems and a distinctive silver-blue hue, is a ubiquitous presence across Aran's desert realms. The Aran use the Desert Whisper to weave intricate baskets and mats, as well as to thatch the roofs of their desert dwellings, the grass's hardy, water-resistant nature making it an invaluable resource in the arid climate.

Desert Oases and their Bounty

While the Aran's desert landscapes are largely dominated by hardy, drought-resistant flora, the planet's oases, fed by underground aquifers, support a lush and diverse array of plant life. Here, the Aran can find the stately Medjool Palm with its broad, fanning leaves and clusters of sweet, nutritious fruit, as well as the fragrant Karna trees, whose wood is prized for its rich, spicy aroma and use in incense and perfumes.

Medjool Palm

Karna Tree

Desert Oases and their Bounty

The oases also play host to a variety of edible plants, such as the succulent Moonmelon, with its thick, juicy rind and sweet, refreshing flesh, and the hardy Desert Spinacia, a spikeless cactus like plant, whose leaves can be harvested and prepared as a nutritious vegetable. These oasis-dwelling plants provide the Aran with a vital source of sustenance and nourishment, helping to sustain their desert civilization.

Moonmelon

Desert Spinacia

The Flora of Zarah: A Delicate Balance

The diverse flora of Zarah is not merely a collection of hardy, desert-adapted. plants; it is a delicate and interconnected ecosystem that is crucial to the survival of the Aran people. From the towering Solarwood trees that provide the raw materials for their crafts to the resilient Sand Whisper that shields their homes, the Aran have developed a deep understanding and reverence for the plants that thrive in their arid world.

By carefully tending to the oases and managing the use of their precious desert resources, the Aran ensure that this fragile balance is maintained, preserving the natural bounty of Zarah for generations to come. The flora of this desert planet is not merely a backdrop to the Aran's civilization, but an integral part of their identity, woven into the very fabric of their culture and traditions.

The Fauna of Zarah

In the vast expanse of the Leander System, on the desert planet of Zarah, the House of Aran stands as a testament to human resilience and adaptation. Descended from the ancient House of Abraxas, the Aran have forged a civilization that not only survives but thrives in the most unforgiving of environments. Unaware of their celestial neighbors on the system's other five planets, the Aran have developed a culture intrinsically bound to the rhythms and challenges of their desert home.

26

Sand Serpents

Serpentine creatures that swim through the dunes like water. Their scaled hides, nearly impenetrable, are highly prized by Aran crafters who fashion them into armour capable of withstanding the harshest sandstorms. The hunting of these creatures is a rite of passage for young warriors, requiring teams of skilled riders on Black Desert Steeds to coordinate their movements with legendary precision.

Dune Stalkers

Multi-legged arachnids wiith exoskeletons that refract sunlight, rendering them nearly invisible in the desert heat. Their razor-sharp claws can slice through almost anything, but when properly treated, make exceptional strings for the famous Sandsong Lutes of the Aran musicians.

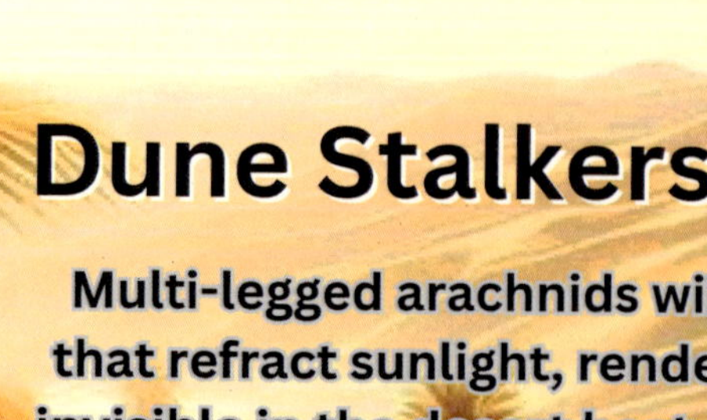

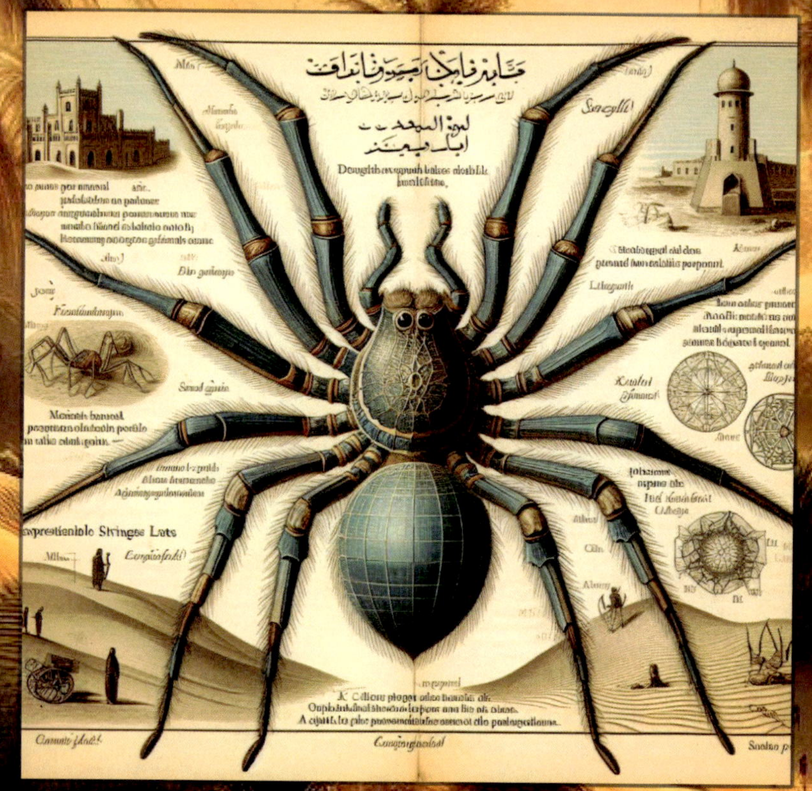

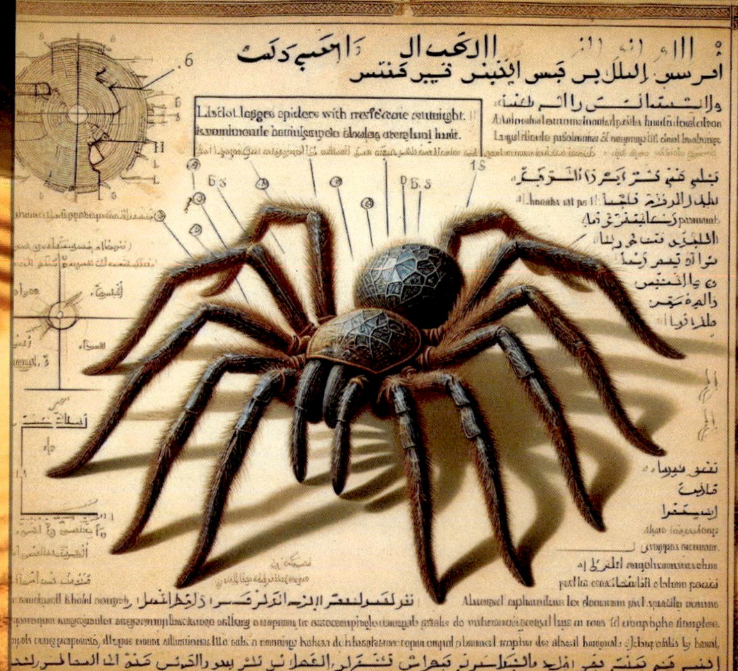

Desert Nightwings

Nocturnal avians with wingspans reaching seven feet. Their feathers absorb moonlight, allowing them to fly silently through the darkness. Aran hunters craft ceremonial cloaks from their plumage, believed to grant the wearer enhanced night vision.

Ocean Dwellers

The seas of Zarah harbour creatures are equally fantastic and fearsome

Crystalline Leviathans

Bioluminescent giants that traverse the depths, their translucent bodies housing organs that produce haunting, melodious sounds. The Aran of the Kingdom of Yara have learned to craft "Ocean Pipes" from their hollow bones, creating instruments that produce otherworldly music said to call to the creatures' distant kin.

Sandfish

Unusual creatures that swim through both water and sand with equal ease. Their iridescent scales are woven into the finest garments worn by Aran nobility, shimmering with an inner light that seems to pulse in rhythm with the wearer's heartbeat.

Craftsmanship and Resource Utilization

The Aran's relationship with Zarah's wildlife exemplifies their philosophy of respectful utilization. Every part of a hunted creature finds purpose

1. Weaponry - The venomous stingers of Dune Scorpions are carefully extracted and used to create poison-tipped arrows. The process is so refined that a single stinger can arm an entire quiver of arrows, each capable of paralyzing a full-grown Sand Serpent.

2. Musical Instruments - The hollow bones of Desert Nightwings form the basis of wind instruments unique to Aran culture. When shaped by master craftsmen, these bones produce notes that seem to carry for miles across the desert, used both in ceremonies and as a sophisticated system of long-distance communication.

3. Textile Arts - The silk-like fibres produced by Sand Weavers, arachnid creatures that build vast underground networks, are harvested to create fabrics of incredible strength and beauty. These textiles, nearly weightless yet capable of turning aside a blade, are so valued that they often serve as currency in major transactions.

The Aran's interaction with Zarah's wildlife has shaped their culture in profound ways

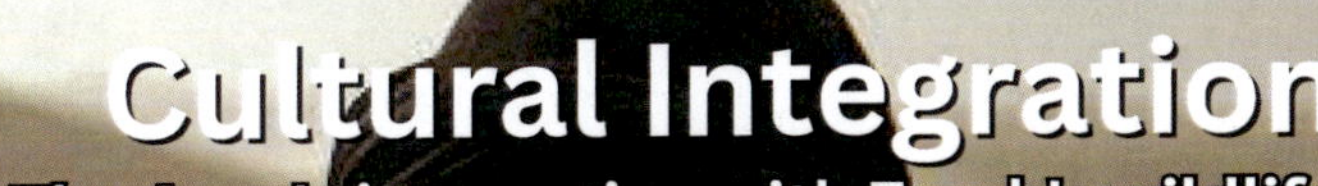

1. The Great Hunt Festival - An annual event in the Kingdom of Arsian where hunters compete to track and subdue (not kill) a juvenile Sand Serpent. The victor earns not only glory but the right to lead the kingdom's hunting parties for the following year.

2. Beastmaster Priests - A specialized sect within the Priesthood of the Sun who communes with Zarah's creatures. They are said to be able to call Sand Serpents from beneath the dunes and calm the fearsome Dune Stalkers with but a whisper.

Encounters With the Creatures of Zarah

The annals of Aran history are replete with tales of extraordinary encounters between the people and the diverse wildlife that inhabit the deserts of Zarah. These interactions, borne of necessity, reverence, and chance, have shaped the Aran's culture, mythology, and worldview in profound ways.

The Serpent's Mercy

During the devastating Great Sandstorm Crisis that swept across Zarah over two centuries ago, Aran caravan found itself stranded in the heart of the Coastal Deserts, battered by howling win and blinding sheets of sand. As the travelers huddled together, resigned to their fate, a massi shape emerged from the roiling sands – a Sand Serpent, its body glowing with an otherworld light.

To the astonishment of the Aran, the colossal creature extended its enormous bulk, envelopi the caravan within the protective confines of its form. The Serpent's bones resonated with haunting, melodic song that seemed to soothe the raging storm, shielding the travelers from t worst of the sandstorm's fury. For three days and three nights, the caravan remained safe with the Serpent's embrace, emerging unscathed when the winds finally subsided.

This extraordinary act of compassion has become a cornerstone of Aran mythology, with t image of the sheltering Leviathan now adorning the royal crest of the House of Aran. The tale recounted with reverence during the annual Sandsong Festival, its melancholic melody inspiri generations of Aran musicians to craft instruments from the bones of these enigmatic sa dwellers.

The Night Queen's Ride

In the tumultuous years following the Great Desert Unification, Queen Amara of Qamar faced the daunting task of consolidating the loyalty of the newly united kingdoms. Recognizing the need for swift, discreet travel between her domains, the Queen turned to an unlikely ally – a massive Desert Nightwing that she had personally tamed through a combination of patience, reverence, and a deep understanding of the creature's nature.

Under the cloak of night, Queen Amara would take to the skies, the Nightwing's silent wings carrying her swiftly between the kingdoms. Legends speak of the Queen's midnight journeys, where she would descend upon unsuspecting settlements, dispensing wisdom, resolving disputes, and reinforcing the bonds of loyalty that held the Aran people together.

The songs composed about these clandestine flights, accompanied by the haunting melodies of Nightwing-bone instruments, are still performed at the annual Sandsong Festival. They serve as a testament to the Queen's cunning, her connection to the desert's denizens, and the crucial role these encounters played in shaping the destiny of the Aran civilization.

The Beastmaster's Audience

In the heart of the Kingdom of Arsian, within the cloistered sanctum of the Priesthood of the Sun, resides a specialized sect known as the Beastmaster Priests. These individuals, through years of meditation, communion, and deep study of Zarah's wildlife, have attained a profound understanding of the desert's creatures, forging a unique bond that transcends the boundaries of species.

It is said that the Beastmasters can summon the great Sand Serpents from their subterranean lairs with but a whispered incantation, the massive reptiles emerging to coil protectively around the priests. In times of crisis, the Beastmasters have been known to call upon these ancient denizens of the dunes, using their towering forms to shield entire settlements from the ravages of sandstorms or to deter the incursions of hostile forces.

Legends speak of the Beastmasters' ability to commune with the Dune Stalkers, their hides rendering them all but invisible in the shimmering desert heat. These fearsome predators, when properly calmed and commanded, have been known to serve as loyal guardians, their razor-sharp claws and preternatural senses providing an added layer of protection to the Aran people.

The Beastmasters' mastery of Zarah's wildlife is a testament to the Aran's deep reverence for the desert realm and their unwavering belief in the sacred interconnectedness of all living things. Their ability to forge these unique bonds has earned them the respect and awe of their fellow Aran, solidifying their status as living embodiments of the desert's ancient wisdom.

A Testament to Adaptability

The relationship between the House of Aran and the wildlife of Zarah is a testament to their adaptability and respect for their environment. Through centuries of careful observation and interaction, they have developed a symbiotic relationship with the creatures of their world, one that enriches their culture and ensures their survival in the unforgiving desert realm. As the House of Tempus observes from beyond the confines of physical reality, they note with approval the balance the Aran have struck between utilizing and preserving the unique ecosystem of their desert home.

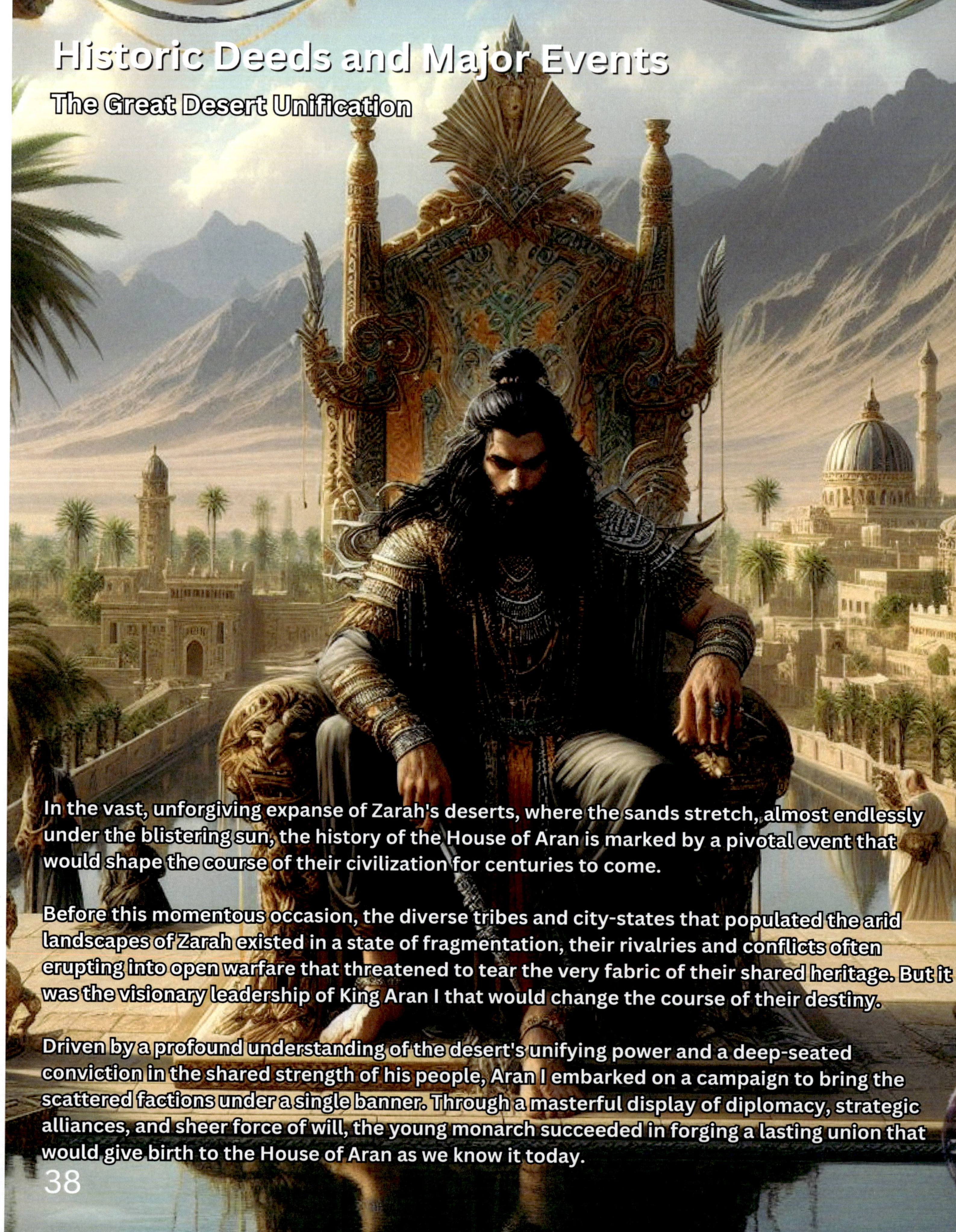

Historic Deeds and Major Events

The Great Desert Unification

In the vast, unforgiving expanse of Zarah's deserts, where the sands stretch, almost endlessly under the blistering sun, the history of the House of Aran is marked by a pivotal event that would shape the course of their civilization for centuries to come.

Before this momentous occasion, the diverse tribes and city-states that populated the arid landscapes of Zarah existed in a state of fragmentation, their rivalries and conflicts often erupting into open warfare that threatened to tear the very fabric of their shared heritage. But it was the visionary leadership of King Aran I that would change the course of their destiny.

Driven by a profound understanding of the desert's unifying power and a deep-seated conviction in the shared strength of his people, Aran I embarked on a campaign to bring the scattered factions under a single banner. Through a masterful display of diplomacy, strategic alliances, and sheer force of will, the young monarch succeeded in forging a lasting union that would give birth to the House of Aran as we know it today.

The Great Desert Unification

The process was neither swift nor easy, as the king and his trusted advisors navigated a complex web of tribal loyalties, regional rivalries, and the ever-present threat of external forces seeking to exploit the divisions within Zarah. But Aran I's unwavering determination, coupled with his keen understanding of the desert's rhythms and the needs of his people, proved to be the decisive factors in his triumph.

As the disparate tribes and kingdoms were slowly united under the Aran banner, the new civilization began to take shape, its identity forged in the crucible of the desert's unforgiving landscape. The six kingdoms that now comprise the House of Aran – Qamar, Shamas, Arsian, Sayf, Kartal, and Yara – each brought their unique cultural and geographical strengths to the table, creating a rich tapestry of traditions, technologies, and military prowess that would serve as the foundation for their future successes.

The Great Desert Unification

The Great Desert Unification was not merely a political or military achievement, but a profound transformation of the Aran's collective consciousness. With the realization of their shared destiny, the people of Zarah embraced a new sense of purpose, one that transcended the petty rivalries of the past and focused instead on the common challenges and aspirations that united them as a people.

In the aftermath of the unification, the Aran set about the task of consolidating their gains, establishing a centralized system of governance, standardizing their military tactics, and fostering a culture of cooperation and mutual respect. The legendary King's Road, a vast network of trade routes and communication lines, was constructed to bind the six kingdoms together, facilitating the exchange of goods, ideas, and cultural traditions that would ultimately strengthen the House of Aran's resilience and prosperity.

The Great Desert Unification

Today, the legacy of the Great Desert Unification echoes across the vast sands of Zarah, a testament to the power of vision, unity, and the indomitable spirit of a people who have learned to thrive in the most unforgiving of environments. The six kingdoms stand as pillars of the Aran civilization, each contributing its unique strengths to the whole, and the memory of King Aran I, the architect of this remarkable transformation, is revered with a reverence that borders on the divine.

For the House of Aran, the Great Desert Unification was not merely a historical event, but a defining moment that forged their identity as a people, a civilization that has proven time and again its ability to overcome the challenges of the desert and emerge stronger, more resilient, and more unified than ever before.

The Siege of Shamas

The Siege of Shamas was a defining moment in Aran history. The Kingdom of Shamas faced a multi-factional siege led by rebellious tribes and external threats. Under the command of General Khalid Al-Rashid, the defenders managed to repel the invaders, a feat that solidified their reputation as skilled tacticians and warriors. The successful defence also showcased their advanced fortifications and military prowess.

The seeds of this conflict were sown centuries ago, when the Kingdom of Shamas, renowned for its solar technology and unparalleled fortifications, began to attract the envy and resentment of its neighbouring kingdoms. Ambitious warlords from the rocky deserts of Sayf, the frigid expanses of Qamar, and even the coastal realms of Yara, eyed Shamas with growing covetousness, eager to seize its wealth and technological advancements for themselves.

The Siege of Shamas

It was the Kingdom of Arsian, however, that struck first, assembling a formidable coalition of disgruntled factions who sought to overthrow the ruling House of Shamas. Driven by a thirst for conquest and the promise of plunder, this motley alliance descended upon the city of Shamaria, intent on bringing the proud kingdom to its knees.

What followed was a grueling siege that would test the mettle of the Aran people like never before. For months, the mighty fortress-city of Shamaria endured a relentless barrage of assaults, as the invading forces hurled wave after wave of warriors, siege engines, and incendiary weapons against its stalwart defenses.

The defenders, led by Khalid Al-Rashid, responded with unwavering determination. From the towering ramparts of the Fortress of the Sun, Aran archers rained down a hail of flaming arrows, while the kingdom's solar-powered artillery pieces unleashed devastating salvos against the besiegers. Beneath the city, teams of engineers worked tirelessly to fortify the extensive network of underground tunnels and fortifications, ensuring that the invaders could not breach the inner sanctum.

The Siege of Shamas

As the siege dragged on, the inhabitants of Shamaria faced mounting hardships. Food and water supplies dwindled, and the echoes of battle reverberated through the streets, shattering the peace that had once defined this cultural hub. Yet, in the face of these challenges, the Aran spirit only grew stronger, as the people of Shamas rallied behind their leaders, determined to defend their home at all costs.

Finally, after months of grueling combat, the tide began to turn. Khalid Al-Rashid, renowned for his unorthodox strategies, orchestrated a daring counterattack, ordering his forces to sally forth from the city's hidden passages and strike the invaders' supply lines. Caught off guard, the besieging army found itself beset by Aran warriors on all sides, their morale crumbling as they watched their comrades fall.

In the end, the Siege of Shamas ended in a decisive victory for the House of Aran. The invading forces, their ranks decimated and their resolve shattered, were forced to retreat, licking their wounds and conceding defeat to the indomitable spirit of the Aran people.

The aftermath of the Siege was a testament to the enduring strength of the House of Aran. The kingdom of Shamas emerged from the conflict bruised but unbroken, its people more united than ever before. The victory also cemented the reputation of the Aran as skilled tacticians and resilient warriors, a reputation that would serve them well in the centuries to come as they faced new challenges and threats to their desert realm.

To this day, the Siege of Shamas is remembered as a pivotal moment in Aran history, a time when the very essence of their civilization was tested, and they emerged victorious, their identity as guardians of the desert realm forever forged in the crucible of battle.

The Desert Accord

In the vast expanse of Zarah's deserts, where the six kingdoms of the House of Aran have carved out their distinct identities and territories, there exists a pivotal agreement that has transcended the boundaries of individual realms and solidified the foundations of their shared civilization. This landmark accord, known as the Desert Accord, stands as a testament to the Aran's unwavering commitment to cooperation, trade, and the preservation of their collective prosperity.

The origins of the Desert Accord can be traced back several centuries, to a time when the disparate kingdoms of Zarah had yet to fully reconcile the rivalries and tensions that had once threatened to tear their world asunder. Recognizing the inherent strength and resilience that could be found in unity, the ruling monarchs and their advisors embarked on a bold initiative to forge a lasting alliance that would benefit all.

The negotiations that led to the Desert Accord were no easy task, as each kingdom sought to protect its own interests and assert its unique cultural and economic priorities. Yet, it was the steady hand of diplomacy, the willingness to compromise, and the overarching vision of a prosperous and harmonious future that ultimately prevailed.

The final terms of the Desert Accord were comprehensive and far-reaching, establishing a framework for the free movement of goods, people, and ideas across the kingdoms. Trade routes were meticulously mapped and secured, ensuring the uninterrupted flow of vital resources, from the sun-drenched oases of Shamas to the frigid northern reaches of Qamar. Additionally, the accord formalized a system of diplomatic relations, with each kingdom appointing ambassadors and envoys to foster cultural exchanges and facilitate the resolution of disputes.

Perhaps most significantly, the Desert Accord laid the groundwork for the technological and scientific advancements that would come to define the House of Aran's golden age. By facilitating the sharing of knowledge and innovations across the kingdoms, the accord enabled the Aran to tackle the formidable challenges of their desert existence with a united front, pooling their collective expertise to develop groundbreaking solutions in areas such as water management, solar energy, and desert fortification.

The Desert Accord

The impact of the Desert Accord cannot be overstated. In the centuries that followed its signing, the Aran civilisation experienced a period of unprecedented prosperity and stability, as the kingdoms worked in concert to not only defend their territories but also to push the boundaries of their cultural, economic, and technological achievements.

The Desert Caravan, a network of heavily fortified trade routes that spanned the length and breadth of Zarah, became a symbol of the accord's success, facilitating the exchange of goods, ideas, and cultural traditions between the disparate realms. The capital cities of each kingdom, once rivals, now thrived as hubs of commerce and innovation, their citizens enjoying the fruits of the accord's success.

Today, the Desert Accord is revered as one of the greatest achievements in Aran history, a testament to the power of cooperation, diplomacy, and a shared vision for a brighter future. Its legacy continues to shape the Aran's collective identity, reminding them of the strength that can be found in unity and the endless possibilities that arise when the kingdoms of Zarah work in harmony.

As the sands of time continue to shift and the challenges of the desert evolve, the Desert Accord remains a guiding light for the House of Aran, a beacon of hope that inspires them to maintain the delicate balance between their individual identities and their shared destiny as the custodians of this remarkable civilisation.

The Great Sandstorm Crisis

A catastrophic sandstorm, known as the Great Sandstorm Crisis, struck Zarah over two centuries ago, devastating large portions of the desert where some kingdoms were situated. The Aran's ability to adapt and rebuild, thanks to their advanced desert technologies, demonstrated their resilience and innovation. This event led to the creation of enhanced sandstorm prediction and mitigation technologies.

The crisis began without warning, as a series of powerful sandstorms swept across the kingdoms of Zarah, their intensity and duration far exceeding anything the Aran had ever witnessed in their history. The relentless onslaught of howling winds, stinging sand, and choking dust quickly overwhelmed the defences of even the most well-fortified cities, leaving devastation in their wake.

Entire settlements were buried beneath the shifting dunes, their inhabitants forced to flee or perish in the unforgiving embrace of the desert. Vital trade routes were severed, and communication between the kingdoms was all but severed, leaving the Aran people isolated and vulnerable.

As the crisis unfolded, the ruling monarchs and their advisors found themselves faced with an unprecedented challenge. The very foundations of their civilization – their mastery of the desert, their technologies, and their intricate network of alliances – seemed to crumble in the face of this natural onslaught.

But the Aran were a people forged in the crucible of adversity, and they were not about to surrender their hard-won way of life without a fight. Across the kingdoms, the populace rallied, their unwavering determination fueling a remarkable display of resilience and innovation. Under the guidance of visionary leaders and the collective wisdom of the Order of the Sacred Desert, the Aran set about the arduous task of rebuilding and reinforcing their defences. New sandstorm prediction and mitigation technologies were developed, drawing upon the ancient knowledge of the desert and the latest advancements in engineering.

The Desert Accord, once a symbol of cooperation and prosperity, now became the linchpin of the Aran's survival strategy, as the kingdoms pooled their resources and expertise to weather the crisis. Trade routes were painstakingly restored, and communication lines were reestablished, allowing the flow of vital supplies and the coordination of relief efforts.

The Great Sandstorm Crisis

In the face of overwhelming odds, the Aran people displayed a level of resilience and resourcefulness that would become the stuff of legend. They rebuilt their shattered cities, replanted their decimated gardens, and restored the delicate balance of their desert ecosystem, all the while maintaining their unwavering dedication to the preservation of their unique cultural heritage.

This crisis was a defining moment in the history of the House of Aran, a testament to their indomitable spirit and their unshakable commitment to the lands they call home. The scars of this catastrophic event still linger, but the Aran have emerged from the ordeal stronger, more unified, and more determined than ever to safeguard their desert realm.

Today, the legacy of the Great Sandstorm Crisis lives on in the minds and hearts of the Aran people, a constant reminder of the power of nature and the unbreakable will of those who have learned to thrive in the most unforgiving of environments.

As the sands of time continue to shift, the Aran stand ready, their ancient wisdom and technological prowess poised to meet any challenge that may arise, ever vigilant in their duty to protect the delicate balance of their desert world.

The Six Kingdoms of the House of Aran

Kingdom of Qamar

Kingdom of Shamas

Kingdom of Arsian

The Six Kingdoms of the House of Aran
Kingdom of Sayf
Kingdom of Kartal
Kingdom of Yara
KINGDOM of YARA
51

The Kingdom of Qamar

Nestled in Zarah's cold deserts, Qamar is a place of quiet reflection, where the pale sands shimmer under the twin moons' soft glow. The landscape is serene, dotted with smooth dunes and jagged outcroppings that cast long shadows across the nighttime terrain. Here, the air is cool, and the sky is awash with stars, creating a mystical atmosphere that permeates every aspect of life. These cold deserts are home of Qamar, the seat of the Aran monarchy. The capital city, Qamaria, is renowned for its grand Royal Citadel, which houses the ruling dynasty and serves as the administrative centre. The kingdom is a hub of political activity and is known for its Great Council of Qamar, where decisions affecting the entirety of Zarah are made. Qamaria is also famous for its Desert Gardens, meticulously maintained oases that serve as a cultural and recreational centre. The people of Qamar are deeply connected to the lunar cycles, their culture shaped by the ebb and flow of celestial rhythms. Temples dedicated to the moon dot the landscape, with tranquil gardens that bloom under the night's gentle light, offering places of meditation and introspection.

The Kingdom of Shamas

On the opposite end of the spectrum to Qamar, lies the Kingdom of Shamas, where the deserts are alive with heat and light. Situated in the subtropical zones, the scorching sun reigns supreme, and the land bakes under its relentless intensity. The people of Shamas have adapted to the extreme conditions, becoming masters of solar energy and heat-resistant technologies. Their cities are marvels of engineering, designed to absorb and harness the sun's heat. Shamas is known for its robust desert fortifications and vibrant cultural festivals. The capital, Shamaria, features the Fortress of the Sun, a formidable defensive structure designed to withstand extreme desert conditions. Shamas is celebrated for the Sandsong Festival, a cultural event that highlights traditional music and dance, including performances with the Desert Drum and Sand Flute. Despite the harsh environment, the people of Shamas are known for their vitality and ingenuity, thriving under conditions that would break lesser beings.

The Kingdom of Arsian

Influenced heavily by the House of Leo, the Arsians are a proud and noble warrior society that rises from Zarah's rugged deserts. Its landscapes are dotted with formidable fortresses and military academies, where the art of war is both studied and perfected. The lion is a revered symbol in Arsian, not just of power but of guardianship and honour. Their cities, fortified with high stone walls and defensive towers, stand ready for any conflict, but they are also adorned with intricate lion motifs - statues and frescoes adorning their halls. Arsian's people are fiercely loyal and courageous, upholding a code of honour that binds them to protect the weak and uphold justice. The Kingdom of Arsian stands as a symbol of martial excellence, a place where warriors are not just trained but forged by the desert's heat and the weight of their lineage. Arsian is also notable for its extensive underground cities, which provide refuge from the harsh desert environment. The city of Arsiana is a subterranean marvel illuminated by bioluminescent fungi and crystal lamps. Arsian art is also characterized by sand mosaics and cave paintings, reflecting their unique cultural and environmental adaptations.

The Kingdom of Sayf

In the unforgiving deserts of jagged rocks and sparse vegetation, the Kingdom of Sayf thrives in an atmosphere of strength, discipline, and a relentless focus on warfare. The land itself is harsh - scorched earth and sharp cliffs that challenge even the hardiest of travellers. Here, the people have built cities that resemble fortresses, their thick stone walls, and iron gates standing as symbols of their resolve. Sayf's culture revolves around the mastery of the sword, and their martial academies are famed throughout Zarah for producing the most skilled tacticians and fighters. Discipline is the cornerstone of Sayf's society, where children are taught the ways of combat from a young age, and every citizen contributes to the military might of the kingdom. Statues of legendary warriors and historical battles line the streets, reminding all of the cost of strength and the honour of defending their homeland. Sayf is known for its advanced irrigation systems and lush desert gardens. True warriors, however, would not be complete merely with martial training. The peoples of Sayf possess as well, a deep connection to natural environment. The capital, Sayfara, is renowned for its Oasis Gardens, a vast complex of greenery and water features. Sayf's culture also emphasizes desert poetry and sand art sculptures, with a strong focus on aesthetic and environmental harmony.

The Kingdom of Kartal

This kingdom is situated high in the rocky deserts. Its cities are built in oasis covered valleys, in between high cliffs, and on top of vast mesas that rise from the desert floor and go on for miles. Kartal's cities are a marvel of engineering, with some offering a breathtaking view of the desert expanse below. The people of Kartal are independent and fierce, with a culture that celebrates the freedom of the skies. Known for their agility and unparalleled skill in archery, the Kartalians model their society after the eagles that soar above them, valuing sharp vision, precision, and independence. Their military forces are swift and deadly, often striking from above like the birds of prey they revere. Kartal is also known for its mastery of high-altitude combat, with their warriors expertly trained in mountain warfare. Kartal is also renowned for its horse culture, with intricate horse gear and craftsmanship, including ornate bridles and saddles adorned with desert motifs.

The Kingdom of Yara

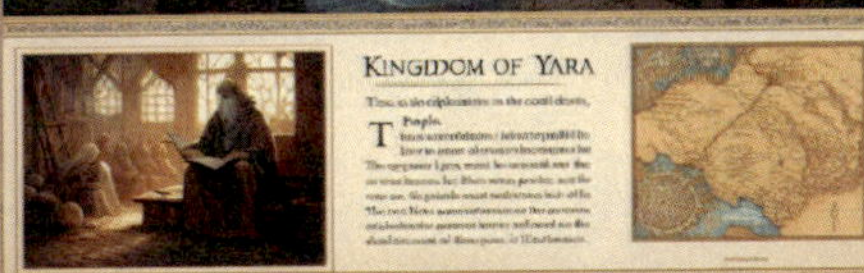

In contrast to the more warlike kingdoms, Yara sits peacefully in the coastal deserts where the sea meets the sands. Yara's people are known for their diplomacy and craftsmanship, and their cities are vibrant hubs of trade and culture. Here, the air is cooler, and the gentle sea breezes offer a reprieve from the desert's harshness. The architecture of Yara reflects its peaceful nature, with open marketplaces, grand fountains, and elegant palaces. Unlike the fortresses of Sayf or Arsian, Yara's cities are built for commerce and community, with wide streets and expansive ports that welcome traders from around Zarah. Known as skilled negotiators and artisans, the people of Yara have a long history of alliance-building and peaceful resolutions, earning them the respect of even the most powerful kingdoms. Their craftsmanship is unrivalled, and their goods - fine textiles, intricate jewellery, and masterfully crafted weapons - are sought after throughout the planet. Yara stands as a beacon of cooperation and hospitality, offering sanctuary and peace to all who pass through its lands. Yara is a kingdom famous for its artistic achievements and ceremonial practices. The capital city, Yararia, features the Artisan's Plaza, a central square showcasing intricate sculptures and mosaics. Yara's culture places a strong emphasis on music and dance, with traditional performances often held in grand amphitheatres.

A Study of Aran Culture

Sand Art - A Canvas Depicting a Guardian of the Sacred Desert

Rock Art - A Depiction of Kartal Warriors

Guardian of the Sacred Desert
61

he priesthood of the Su
was somewhere betwee
the desert realm of Zerrah.
The Priesthood of the Sun
62

Monument of the Old Kings

The Great Desert Race

Kingdom of Sayf
66

Guardian of the Sacred Desert - Kingdom of Sayf

The Priesthood of the Sun
68

Statues of Rafiq and King Aran I

Kingdom of Arsian
70

The Great Sandstorm Crisis

Aran Culture and Society

In the vast, unforgiving expanse of Zarah's deserts, where the peoples of the House of Aran have carved their enduring legacy, the noble steed stands as a revered and indispensable companion, a testament to the deep, abiding bond that has shaped the very fabric of their civilization. For the Aran, the horse is not merely a mode of transportation or a tool of warfare, but a living embodiment of their indomitable spirit, their unwavering resilience, and their profound connection to the land they call home.

Equestrian Culture: The House of Aran's equestrian culture is a cornerstone of their society. Their horses, particularly the Black Desert Steed, are adapted to the harsh desert environment and are central to their way of life. The Great Desert Race held annually in Qamar is a significant cultural event, demonstrating the Aran's breeding and riding expertise.

The process of breeding and training the Black Desert Steed is a deeply revered tradition, passed down through the generations with meticulous care and attention to detail. Aran breeders, drawing upon centuries of accumulated knowledge and keen observation of the desert's rhythms, meticulously select and pair their breeding stock, ensuring that each successive generation inherits the qualities that have made their horses the envy of all who witness them.

The training of these remarkable steeds is no less an art form, requiring a profound understanding of the animal's instincts, temperament, and physical capabilities. Aran horse masters, themselves skilled riders and trainers, work in close harmony with their equine charges, forging an unbreakable bond through a combination of patience, gentle guidance, and an unwavering respect for the horse's inherent dignity and autonomy.

The result of this painstaking process is a breed of horse that is truly unlike any other, possessing not only the physical prowess to navigate the treacherous terrain of Zarah's deserts but also a profound, almost intuitive, understanding of the needs and rhythms of their Aran riders. These horses are trusted companions, loyal allies, and, in the eyes of the Aran, living embodiments of the very spirit that defines their civilization.

Aran Horse Culture

The centrality of the horse to Aran culture is perhaps best exemplified in the annual Great Desert Race, a breathtaking spectacle that draws crowds from across the six kingdoms to witness the unparalleled skills of the Aran's equestrian masters. As the thundering hooves echo across the sands, the riders and their noble steeds become a single, unified force, their movements flowing with a grace and synchronicity that defies the very laws of nature.

But the significance of the horse in Aran society extends far beyond the realm of sport and warfare. These majestic creatures are deeply revered in the spiritual and cultural traditions of the Aran people, their very presence imbued with symbolic meaning and metaphysical power. In the rituals overseen by the Order of the Sacred Desert, the Black Desert Steed is seen as a conduit to the divine, a living connection to the desert's primal forces and the celestial rhythms that govern the Aran's world.

As the sands of Zarah continue to shift and the winds of change blow across the kingdoms, the enduring legacy of the Aran horse culture remains a steadfast pillar of their civilization. The Black Desert Steed, with its unparalleled strength, speed, and loyalty, has become a symbol of the Aran's indomitable spirit, a living embodiment of the resilience and adaptability that have allowed this remarkable people to thrive in the most unforgiving of environments.

In the thunderous hoofbeats and the graceful movements of these noble creatures, the Aran people glimpse the very essence of their shared destiny, a bond that transcends the boundaries of the material world and connects them to the timeless rhythms of the desert they call home.
These horses are revered as companions, often treated as members of the family. It is said that an Aran warrior is never truly alone as long as they have their steed by their side.

The Great Desert Race

Held annually in Qamar, it is one of the most significant cultural and sporting events in the Aran calendar. Riders from all six kingdoms compete in a gruelling race across the desert, testing their skills, endurance, and the strength of their steeds. Victory in this race brings great honour, and the winning rider is often showered with gifts and recognition from the royal families.

This annual spectacle, a testament to the Aran's unparalleled equestrian prowess and their deep, abiding connection to the land they call home, is a celebration of speed, endurance, and the indomitable spirit that has defined their civilization for generations.

The Great Desert Race begins in the shimmering splendor of Qamaria, the capital city of the Kingdom of Qamar, where the Royal Palace stands as a silent witness to the gathering of riders and their noble steeds. Across the kingdom, the people have gathered, lining the streets and filling the grand amphitheaters, their anticipation palpable as they await the thundering hooves that will soon echo across the sands.

At the sound of the ceremonial horn, the riders surge forth, their Black Desert Steeds surging with a primal power that sends shivers down the spines of all who behold them. The riders, their faces set with a fierce determination, guide their mounts through the treacherous terrain, navigating the shifting dunes, rocky ravines, and the ever-present threat of sandstorms that seek to impede their progress.

As the race unfolds, the spectators are swept up in a frenzy of excitement, their cheers and chants echoing across the desert landscape. For the Aran, this is more than just a test of speed and endurance; it is a celebration of their deep-rooted connection to the land and the noble creatures that have become an integral part of their way of life.

The riders, their bodies in perfect harmony with their mounts, weave through the obstacles with a grace and agility that defies the very laws of nature. They are the embodiment of the Aran spirit, their skill and determination honed through generations of mastering the harsh realities of their desert home.

The Great Desert Race

As the race reaches its climactic conclusion, the riders push their steeds to their limits, their muscles straining and their lungs burning with the exertion. The thunderous hoofbeats reverberate across the sands, sending a shockwave of anticipation through the gathered throngs.

In the end, it is the rider who crosses the finish line first, their steed's nostrils flaring and their mane whipping in the desert wind, who is crowned the champion of the Great Desert Race. The victor is showered with accolades, their name etched into the annals of Aran history, destined to be remembered and revered for generations to come.

But the true triumph of the Great Desert Race lies not in the crowning of a single champion, but in the celebration of the Aran's indomitable spirit, their unwavering connection to the land, and their mastery of the noble creatures that have become the very symbol of their civilization. For in the spectacle of this grand event, the Aran people affirm their enduring legacy, their unbreakable bond with the desert that has shaped their destiny, and their unyielding determination to conquer the challenges that lie ahead.

Horses are also integral to the military strategies of the peoples of Aran. The cavalry of Qamar, mounted on their Black Desert Steeds, is one of the most feared forces on Zarah. They are known for their ability to strike quickly and retreat into the vast expanse of the desert before their enemies can even react. Cavalry tactics have been refined over centuries, making the Aran a formidable power in both defence and offence.

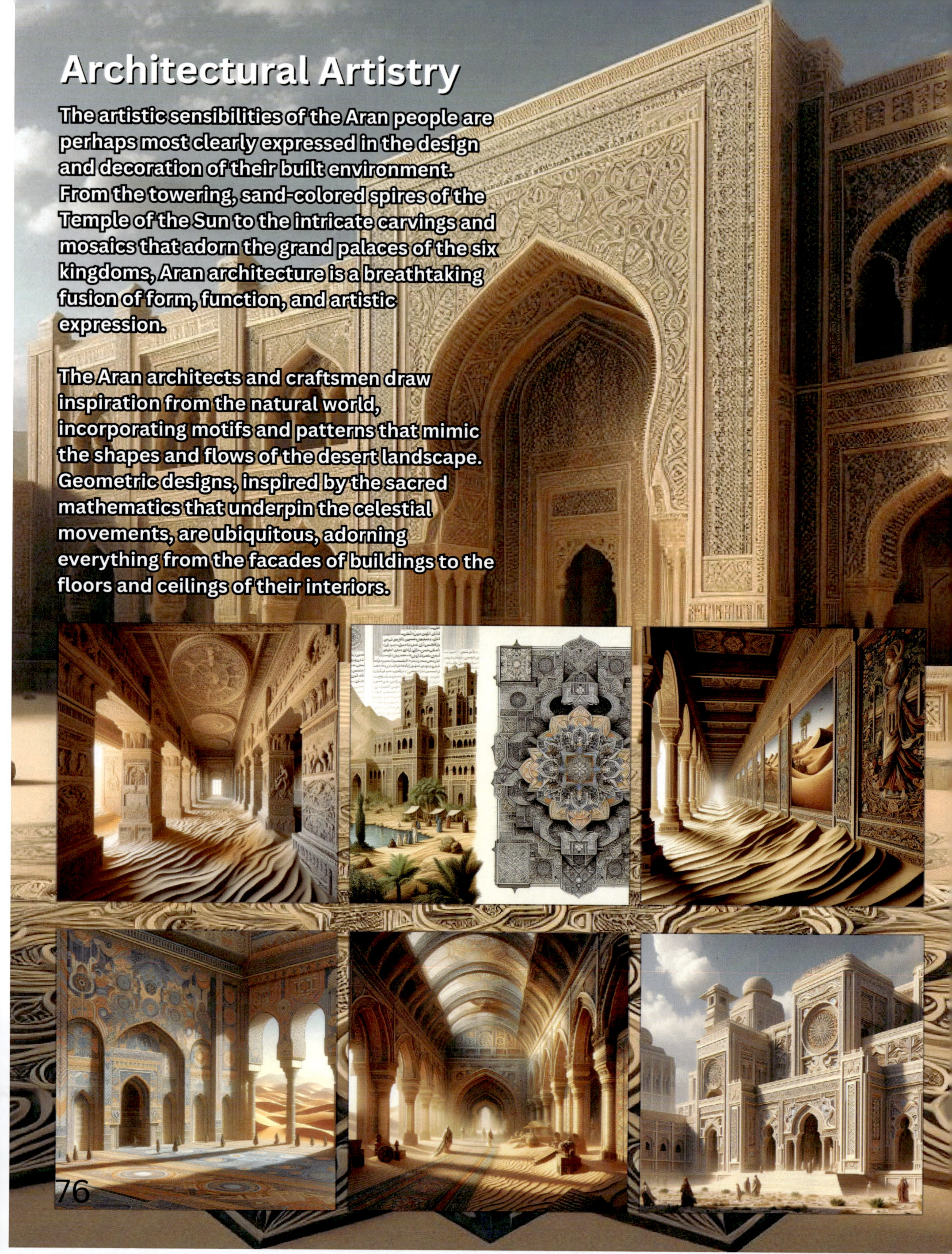

Architectural Artistry

The artistic sensibilities of the Aran people are perhaps most clearly expressed in the design and decoration of their built environment. From the towering, sand-colored spires of the Temple of the Sun to the intricate carvings and mosaics that adorn the grand palaces of the six kingdoms, Aran architecture is a breathtaking fusion of form, function, and artistic expression.

The Aran architects and craftsmen draw inspiration from the natural world, incorporating motifs and patterns that mimic the shapes and flows of the desert landscape. Geometric designs, inspired by the sacred mathematics that underpin the celestial movements, are ubiquitous, adorning everything from the facades of buildings to the floors and ceilings of their interiors.

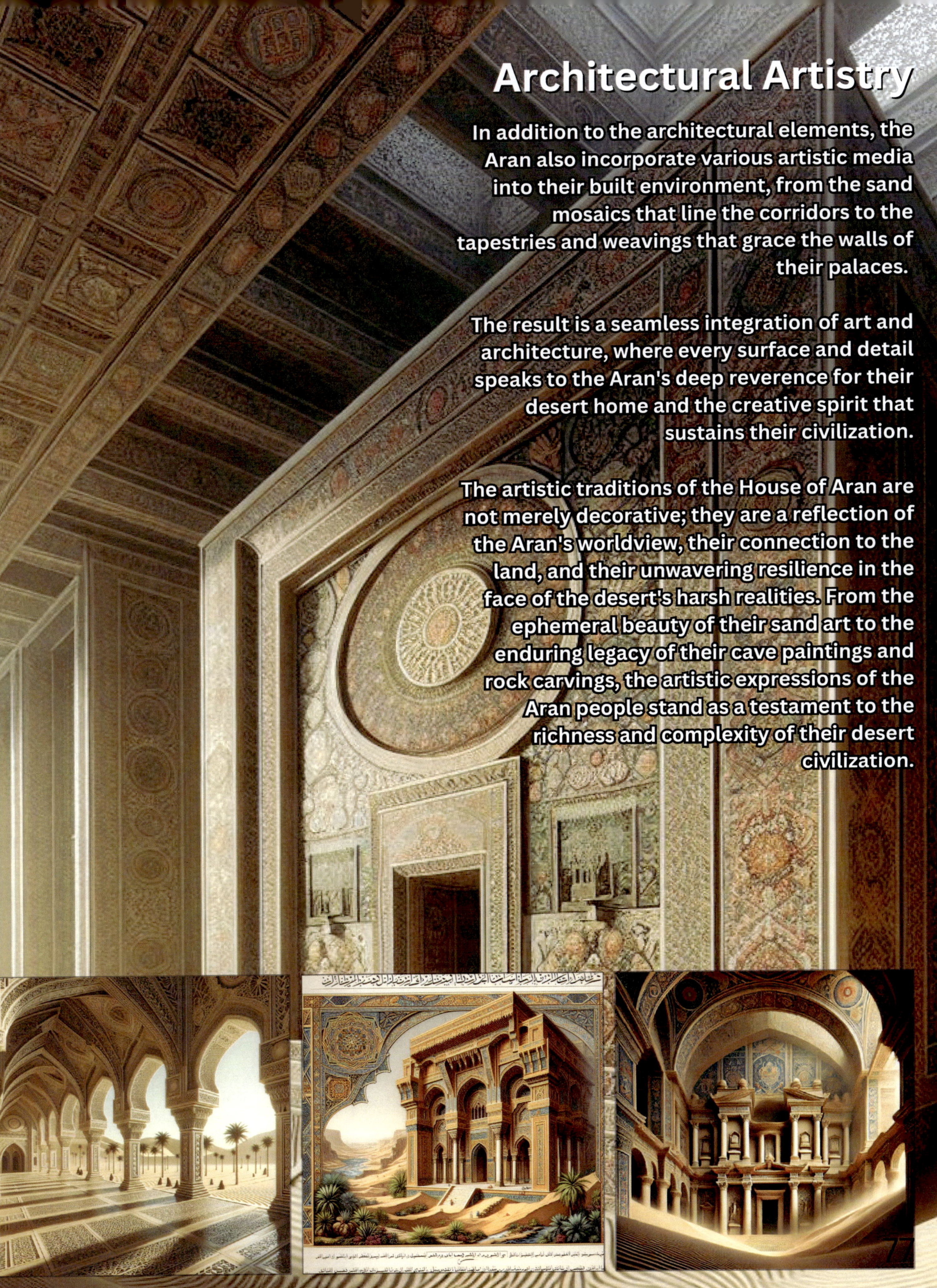

Architectural Artistry

In addition to the architectural elements, the Aran also incorporate various artistic media into their built environment, from the sand mosaics that line the corridors to the tapestries and weavings that grace the walls of their palaces.

The result is a seamless integration of art and architecture, where every surface and detail speaks to the Aran's deep reverence for their desert home and the creative spirit that sustains their civilization.

The artistic traditions of the House of Aran are not merely decorative; they are a reflection of the Aran's worldview, their connection to the land, and their unwavering resilience in the face of the desert's harsh realities. From the ephemeral beauty of their sand art to the enduring legacy of their cave paintings and rock carvings, the artistic expressions of the Aran people stand as a testament to the richness and complexity of their desert civilization.

Monuments

Amidst the vast, unforgiving expanse of Zarah's deserts, the peoples of the House of Aran have left an indelible mark upon the rugged landscape, etching their storied history into the very stone and sand that define their realm. Where other civilizations might have succumbed to the relentless march of the elements, the Aran have risen to the challenge, harnessing the harsh beauty of their world to craft monuments of breathtaking grandeur.

These great structures, carved directly into the towering cliffs and towering mountainsides, stand as testaments to the ingenuity, resilience, and reverence of the Aran people. Figures of legendary heroes and ancestral deities gaze out over the endless dunes, their weathered features bearing witness to the trials and triumphs that have shaped the destiny of this remarkable civilization.

The great statue of King Aran I, the unifier who forged the disparate tribes into a singular, formidable House, rises from the base of the Crimson Cliffs, its immense form casting a long shadow over the bustling oasis city of Qamaria. The king's outstretched arm seems to beckon travelers and conquerors alike, a silent challenge to those who would dare to test the mettle of his descendants.

Elsewhere, in the shadow of the Shattered Mountains, the Aran have carved a pantheon of their revered deities, each figure hewn from the living rock with a level of detail that defies the limitations of mortal hands. The leonine visage of the Sun God, Tarek, gazes impassively over the scorched sands, while the serene countenance of the Moon Goddess, Alya, watches over the more contemplative inhabitants of the frigid northern deserts. Many Aran artists have attempted to depict this monument in their respective crafts.

Monuments

Perhaps the most awe-inspiring of these monumental works can be found in the heartland of the Kingdom of Arsian, where the towering figures of legendary Aran warriors stand guard over the strategically vital fortresses and military academies that dot the rugged terrain. These colossal statues, their features etched with an unwavering determination, serve as a constant reminder to both ally and foe of the martial prowess that flows through the veins of the Aran people.

The creation of these grand monuments is no simple feat, for the Aran have elevated the art of stone carving to a level that rivals the finest sculptors of any civilization, past or present. Teams of skilled artisans, working in concert with architects and engineers, toil for years to bring these visions to life, using intricate pulley systems and precisely calibrated tools to carve away the unyielding rock, revealing the regal visages and imposing forms that will stand the test of time.

Yet, these monuments are more than mere displays of power and prestige; they are living, breathing embodiments of the Aran's deep-rooted connection to their ancestral past and the unforgiving landscape that has shaped their culture. Each carving, each intricate detail, is imbued with the stories and traditions that have been passed down through generations, serving as a tangible link between the present and the distant, mythic origins of the House of Aran.

As the wind-worn sands of Zarah continue their endless dance, the colossal figures that adorn the planet's mountainsides and cliff faces stand as eternal guardians, reminding all who gaze upon them of the indomitable spirit and unwavering determination that has come to define the peoples of this remarkable civilization. For in the shadow of these monumental works, the legacy of the House of Aran endures, a testament to the power of the desert and the unbreakable will of those who call it home.

Music and Art

In the vast, sun-drenched expanse of Zarah, where the peoples of the House of Aran have carved their enduring legacy, the rhythmic pulse of music echoes across the shifting dunes, weaving a tapestry of culture, tradition, and the very essence of this remarkable civilization. For the Aran, music is not merely a form of entertainment, but a profound expression of their deep-rooted connection to the desert that has shaped their destiny.

At the heart of the Aran musical tradition lies the ancient and revered Desert Drum, a distinctive percussive instrument whose primal beats have reverberated through the centuries, summoning the faithful to sacred ceremonies and rallying the warriors to battle. Crafted from the weathered hides of the mighty desert creatures and with a resonant, earthy tone, the Desert Drum is more than just a mere instrument – it is a living, breathing embodiment of the Aran's enduring spirit.

Accompanying the pulsing rhythms of the Desert Drum are the haunting, ethereal melodies of the Sand Flute, a delicate wind instrument whose reedy tones evoke the whispers of the desert winds and the eternal cycles of life and death. In the hands of a skilled Aran musician, the Sand Flute becomes a vessel for the expression of profound emotions, from the soaring triumph of victory to the mournful lament of those who have fallen in battle.

The House of Aran's musical traditions are also deeply rooted in a rich heritage of string instruments, each one uniquely crafted to capture the essence of the desert realms. These evocative instruments not only provide the foundation for Aran's captivating music but also serve as symbols of their cultural identity and connection to the land.

At the heart of the Aran string ensemble is the Desert Lute, a majestic instrument that has become synonymous with the musical traditions of this desert civilization. Crafted from carefully selected woods and adorned with intricate carvings and inlays, the Desert Lute is a true work of art, its very form mirroring the undulating dunes and shifting sands of Zarah.

The instrument's distinctive long neck and rounded, resonant body are perfectly suited to the arid climate, allowing it to project its soulful, melancholic tones across the vast desert expanse. Skilled Aran lute players coax out hauntingly beautiful melodies by plucking the taut strings with their calloused fingers, their virtuosic performances evoking the timeless rhythms of the desert.

The Desert Lute is not merely a musical instrument, but a conduit for the Aran's rich storytelling tradition. Legendary tales of love, loss, and triumph are woven into the very fabric of the music, each note and phrase carrying the weight of the Aran's cultural heritage. As the lute's resonant notes drift across the sands, they serve as a powerful reminder of the enduring spirit of this desert civilization.

Music and Art

Complementing the deep, emotive tones of the Desert Lute is the mesmerizing Sand Harp, an instrument that captures the ephemeral beauty of the desert itself. Crafted from the finest desert hardwoods and adorned with delicate inlays of polished stone and desert glass, the Sand Harp's arched frame and taut, resonant strings create a sound that is both haunting and transcendent.

Unlike the Desert Lute, the Sand Harp is played by plucking or stroking the strings with the fingers, allowing the musician to coax out a shimmering, ethereal quality that evokes the gentle whispers of the desert wind. The instrument's unique tonal characteristics, ranging from the deep, resonant bass to the delicate, crystalline treble, are perfectly suited to the Aran's elaborate musical compositions, which often incorporate elements of celestial cycles and natural rhythms.

The Sand Harp is not merely a musical instrument but a sacred object, imbued with deep spiritual significance for the Aran people. In religious ceremonies and rituals, the haunting melodies of the Sand Harp are used to invoke the blessings of the desert deities and to facilitate deep states of meditation and introspection. The instrument's delicate, ephemeral nature is a potent metaphor for the fragility of life in the desert, and the Aran's unwavering dedication to preserving the balance of their harsh, yet beautiful, environment.

Rounding out the Aran's string instrument ensemble is the Desert Zither, a uniquely shaped instrument that draws inspiration from the rugged, angular landscapes of Zarah. Crafted from sturdy desert hardwoods and adorned with intricate geometric patterns, the Desert Zither's distinctive trapezoidal frame and taut, resonant strings produce a bold, percussive sound that complements the more melodic tones of the Desert Lute and Sand Harp.

Aran zither players are renowned for their virtuosic performances, their nimble fingers dancing across the strings to create complex, rhythmic patterns that evoke the relentless march of the desert wind and the thunderous rumble of distant sandstorms. The instrument's percussive qualities also lend themselves well to the Aran's vibrant, celebratory music, adding a sense of urgency and energy to their traditional dance performances and ceremonial rituals.

Like the other string instruments of the Aran, the Desert Zither is more than just a musical tool; it is a physical embodiment of the desert's enduring spirit. The instrument's rugged construction and bold, unyielding tones reflect the Aran's own unwavering resilience in the face of the harsh realities of their desert home, serving as a symbol of their unwavering determination to preserve their unique cultural heritage.

Together, these instruments form the foundation of the Aran musical tradition, their harmonies weaving a tapestry of sound that is as diverse and captivating as the landscapes that define their world. From the sombre, contemplative melodies that echo through the frigid northern deserts of Qamar to the celebratory, high-energy rhythms that reverberate through the sun-drenched streets of Shamas, the Aran musical repertoire is a living, evolving testament to the richness and complexity of their culture.

Music and Art

But the Aran's musical legacy extends far beyond the boundaries of their traditional instruments, for they have also embraced the transformative power of vocal harmonies. The Sandsong Festival, held annually in the kingdom of Shamas, is a breathtaking display of vocal virtuosity, as singers from across Zarah gather to perform ancient ballads and new compositions that celebrate the Aran's proud history and their unbreakable bond with the desert.

These stirring vocal performances, accompanied by the thunderous beats of the Desert Drum and the haunting melodies of the Sand Flute, have the power to captivate and inspire all who bear witness. The lyrics, rich in metaphor and symbolism, weave intricate tapestries of myth and legend, transporting the audience to the very heart of the Aran's spiritual and cultural identity.

Yet, the significance of music in the House of Aran extends far beyond mere entertainment or artistic expression. In the rituals and ceremonies overseen by the Order of the Sacred Desert, music serves as a conduit to the divine, a means of communing with the very spirit of the desert and invoking the blessings of the celestial bodies that govern their world.

The rhythmic pulsations of the Desert Drum, for example, are believed to mimic the beating heart of the desert itself, synchronizing the worshipper's own spirit with the eternal rhythms of the land. Similarly, the plaintive notes of the Sand Flute are said to carry the whispers of the desert winds, conveying the messages of the desert's guardian deities to the faithful.

In this way, the Aran's musical traditions have become inextricably woven into the fabric of their civilization, serving as a bridge between the material and the ethereal, the physical and the metaphysical. As the sands of Zarah continue to shift and the winds of change blow across the kingdoms, the enduring power of Aran music remains a constant, a guiding light that illuminates the path forward and sustains the unbreakable bond between the people and the land they call home.

Music and Art
The Crafting of Musical Instruments

In the vast expanse of Zarah's deserts, where the peoples of the House of Aran have honed their mastery of the elements, the creation of their revered musical instruments is an art form that transcends the merely functional, imbuing each carefully crafted piece with a deep spiritual and cultural significance.

At the heart of this remarkable tradition are the skilled artisans, whose steady hands and keen eyes transform the raw materials of the desert into the iconic instruments that have become synonymous with the Aran's rich musical heritage. From the thunderous Desert Drum to the hauntingly beautiful Sand Flute, each instrument is a testament to the ingenuity, attention to detail, and reverence that define the Aran's approach to their craft.

The creation of musical instruments within the House of Aran is a meticulous and deeply revered process, imbued with cultural significance and a profound connection to the desert realm. Each instrument is crafted with great care and attention to detail, reflecting the Aran's mastery of their arid environment and their unwavering dedication to preserving their musical traditions.

Music and Art
The Materials of the Desert

At the heart of the Aran's instrument-making lies a deep understanding and appreciation of the natural resources found within the deserts of Zarah. The Aran artisans carefully select the finest desert hardwoods to serve as the foundations for their instruments. These woods are prized for their strength, durability, and resonant properties, qualities that are essential for the creation of instruments capable of withstanding the harsh desert climate.

In addition to the carefully chosen woods, the Aran also incorporate a variety of other natural materials into their instrument designs, including desert grasses, animal hides, and even precious minerals and stones. These elements not only lend a distinctive aesthetic to the finished products but also imbue the instruments with symbolic significance, reflecting the Aran's deep reverence for the land and its bounty.

Music and Art
The Ritual of Instrument Making

The process of creating an Aran musical instrument is itself a sacred ritual, steeped in tradition and spiritual significance. The artisans responsible for this task are highly respected members of the community, their skills and knowledge passed down through generations. Before beginning the intricate process of shaping and assembling the instrument, the craftsmen will engage in meditative practices, aligning themselves with the rhythms and energies of the desert.

The actual construction of the instrument is a methodical and painstaking endeavor, with each step imbued with symbolic meaning. The selection of the raw materials is guided by astrological omens and the counsel of the Priesthood of the Sun, ensuring that the final product will be imbued with the blessing of the desert deities. The shaping and finishing of the instrument are carried out with great care, using specialized tools and techniques that have been refined over centuries of practice.

At critical junctures in the process, the artisans will perform rituals and offer prayers, invoking the protection and guidance of the desert spirits. The very act of stringing and tuning the instrument is seen as a sacred rite, with the musicians carefully adjusting the tension and pitch to align with the cosmic cycles that govern the desert realm.

Music and Art
The Finished Instrument: A Vessel of Culture

Once the instrument has been crafted, it is not merely a functional tool but a vessel for the Aran's rich cultural heritage. The intricate carvings, inlays, and decorative elements adorning the instruments are not merely aesthetic choices, but rather, they are imbued with deep symbolic meaning, referencing the Aran's mythology, their celestial beliefs, and their intimate connection to the desert landscape.

The Desert Lute, for example, may feature delicate etchings depicting the mythical desert creatures that roam the sands, while the Sand Harp's frame might be adorned with intricate mosaic patterns that mirror the shifting dunes. These artistic flourishes serve not only to beautify the instrument but also to imbue it with a sense of cultural identity and spiritual significance.

When the Aran musicians take up their instruments, they do so with a deep reverence for the traditions and beliefs that have shaped these remarkable creations. The very act of playing becomes a ritual in itself, with the musicians drawing upon the instrument's inherent powers to conjure the timeless melodies and rhythms that lie at the heart of Aran culture.

In this way, the Aran's musical instruments serve as living embodiments of their desert civilization, reflecting the ingenuity, artistry, and spiritual devotion that have sustained their people through the endless cycles of the desert. Each note, each resonant vibration, carries the weight of centuries of history, weaving a tapestry of sound that transports the listener into the very essence of the Aran's world.

The creation of the Desert Drum, perhaps the most emblematic of all Aran instruments, begins with the procurement of the raw materials – the weathered hides of mighty desert creatures. These hardy, resilient skins are carefully selected and prepared, undergoing a meticulous process of tanning and curing that imbues them with the necessary tensile strength and resonance to produce the instrument's distinctive, earth-shaking tones.

The drum's frame, meanwhile, is crafted from the sturdy, desert-hardened wood from a native species renowned for its durability and resistance to the elements. Using traditional techniques passed down through generations, the Aran artisans carefully shape and assemble the frame, ensuring that it is perfectly balanced and capable of withstanding the rigors of both performance and the harsh desert environment.
The final stage of the Desert Drum's creation is the application of the prepared hide, a process that requires the utmost precision and skill. The hide is stretched and secured to the frame, its tension carefully adjusted to achieve the desired timbre and resonance. This delicate task is often accompanied by intricate decorative patterns, etched or painted onto the hide, that reflect the cultural motifs and spiritual symbolism associated with the instrument

Music and Art
The Finished Instrument: A Vessel of Culture

The Sand Flute, with its haunting and ethereal tones, represents a different challenge for the Aran craftsmen. These slender, reed-like instruments are fashioned from the hardy stalks of the Desert Cane, a resilient plant that thrives in the arid landscapes of Zarah. Each flute is painstakingly carved and shaped, with the artisans using specialized tools to meticulously bore the precise holes and contours that will give the instrument its distinctive voice.

In addition to the technical mastery required, the creation of the Sand Flute also demands a deep understanding of the desert's natural rhythms and the spiritual significance of the instrument. The positioning and spacing of the finger holes, for example, are often guided by the phases of the moon and the celestial alignments that hold such profound meaning for the Aran people.

The final touches on both the Desert Drum and the Sand Flute involve the application of intricate decorative elements, from delicate inlays and etchings to the incorporation of precious desert-dwelling materials, such as shimmering sand or crushed gemstones. These embellishments are not merely decorative, but rather imbued with symbolic meaning, connecting the instrument to the spiritual and cultural traditions of the Aran civilization.

As the finished instruments are reverently passed from the artisans' workshops to the musicians who will bring them to life, the true essence of the Aran's musical heritage is revealed. For in the creation of these remarkable tools, the people of this desert realm have not only harnessed the natural resources of their environment but also imbued them with a deep, abiding reverence for the land and the timeless rhythms that have sustained their civilization for generations.

In the thunderous beats of the Desert Drum and the haunting melodies of the Sand Flute, the Aran people hear the very heartbeat of their world, a connection to the desert that transcends the physical and taps into the profound spiritual and cultural foundations that define their identity. And in the skilled hands of the artisans who craft these instruments, that connection is forged anew, ensuring that the music of the House of Aran will continue to echo across the sands for centuries to come.

Aran Music
A Celebration of Life

"The Sound of the Desert"

The sands where the winds weave,
A song is born as the deserts breathe.
From the drum's deep pulse to the flute's soft cry,
Each note ascends to kiss the sky.

The lute's strings hum of hearts unchained,
Of struggles faced and triumphs gained.
The harp's sweet voice, a gentle stream,
Carries hope's light through the harsh sunbeam.

In every rhythm, life's essence flows,
The shifting dunes, the moonlight's glow.
A hymn to time, both swift and vast,
A bridge to futures, ties to past.

Oh, Aran's music, sacred art,
You cradle the soul, you heal the heart.
A celebration, fierce and free,
Of life's bold dance in eternity.

88

Zarah's Eternal Song

Beneath the suns' scorching gaze,
Where sands eternal shift and blaze,
The House of Aran lifts its voice,
A hymn of life, a sacred choice.

Through deserts vast where echoes play,
Their music winds a timeless way.
The Desert Drum, with thunderous might,
Beats heartbeats deep, both day and night.
Its cadence calls to life anew,
A primal pulse, both fierce and true.

The Sand Flute's whisper, soft and clear,
Summons the winds that wander near.
Its mournful tones, like whispers pale,
Tell ancient tales through moonlit veils.
A voice of yearning, wild and free,
That charts the path of destiny.

The Desert Lute, with strings of gold,
Sings of heroes, brave and bold.
Its melodies, both bright and grave,
Weave tales of those who dared and gave.
It knows the love that deserts hold,
The fleeting joys, the dreams untold.

And then the Harp of Shifting Sands,
Its chords like waves through timeless lands.
With fingers deft, it plucks the air,
Binding spirits in its snare.
Each note a spark, each tone a fire,
A flame to lift, to reach, inspire.

Their music flows through every dune,
Through Qamar's frost and Shamas' noon.
It dances high where Kartal soars,
And hums in Yara's bustling shores.
In Sayf's hard stone and Arsian pride,
Its echoes never fade or hide.

For every beat, a life reclaimed,
For every chord, a soul unchained.
The music of Aran transcends,
Where hardship starts, and beauty bends.

A celebration vast and grand,
Born of the heart, shaped by the land.
Its rhythms breathe where hope is sown,
A living hymn to all they've known.

Thus, Zarah sings through Aran's art,
A melody to heal the heart.
A truth eternal, fierce, divine.
That life, through song, will ever shine.

Artistic Achievements
Crafting Beauty from the Sands

Art is an integral part of Aran society, and the desert provides endless inspiration for their creativity. The Aran artisans are renowned for their ability to work with the materials of their environment—sand, stone, bone, and metals—to create works of stunning beauty and complexity. Aran art features poetry, sand carvings, stone sculptures, and desert weavings. Their artistic expressions often depict desert scenes and historical events.

The House of Aran has a rich and diverse artistic tradition that reflects the unique character of their desert civilization. From the intricate geometrical patterns adorning their architecture to the evocative sand art sculptures that capture the essence of the shifting sands, the artistic expressions of the Aran people are deeply rooted in their connection to the land and their way of life.

Sand Carving: An art unique to the Aran, sand carving involves creating intricate patterns and designs in large slabs of desert sandstone. These carvings are often ceremonial, used to commemorate significant events or honor important figures. The most famous of these is The Great Desert Unification, a massive carving that depicts the unification of the Aran tribes under King Aran I.

Sand Art and Mosaics

One of the most iconic art forms of the Aran is their breathtaking sand art and mosaics. Using the very sands of Zarah as their canvas, Aran artists create elaborate, ephemeral sculptures and patterns that mimic the natural shapes and flows of the desert. These works often depict scenes from Aran mythology, historical events, or the rhythms of daily life in the desert kingdoms.

The process of creating sand art is a carefully choreographed ritual, requiring precise control of the sands and a deep understanding of the desert's ever-changing moods. Artists will meticulously layer different colored sands, using tools like wooden rakes and their own hands to sculpt the intricate designs. The finished pieces are often displayed in public spaces or used to adorn the floors of temples and palaces, only to be swept away by the next desert wind, leaving behind the memory of their fleeting beauty.

In addition to free-standing sand sculptures, the Aran also incorporate sand mosaics into their architecture, using the medium to decorate the walls, floors, and ceilings of their buildings. These mosaics often feature geometric patterns inspired by the celestial movements and the mathematical principles that underpin the desert environment.

Desert Poetry and Music

The arid landscapes of Zarah have also given rise to a rich tradition of poetry and music within the House of Aran. Aran poets, known for their mastery of rhyme and meter, weave lyrical tales that capture the grandeur, harshness, and ever-changing moods of the desert.

These poems often draw inspiration from the natural world, exploring themes of survival, spirituality, and the eternal human struggle against the unforgiving elements.

Aran music, too, is deeply rooted in the rhythms and sounds of the desert. Instruments like the Desert Drum, crafted from the hides of desert animals, and the haunting Sand Flute, whose melodies evoke the whispers of the wind, are the foundation of Aran musical traditions.

These instruments, along with chants and vocal harmonies, are integral to Aran cultural celebrations and religious ceremonies, creating a sonic landscape that reflects the sacred connection between the people and their environment.

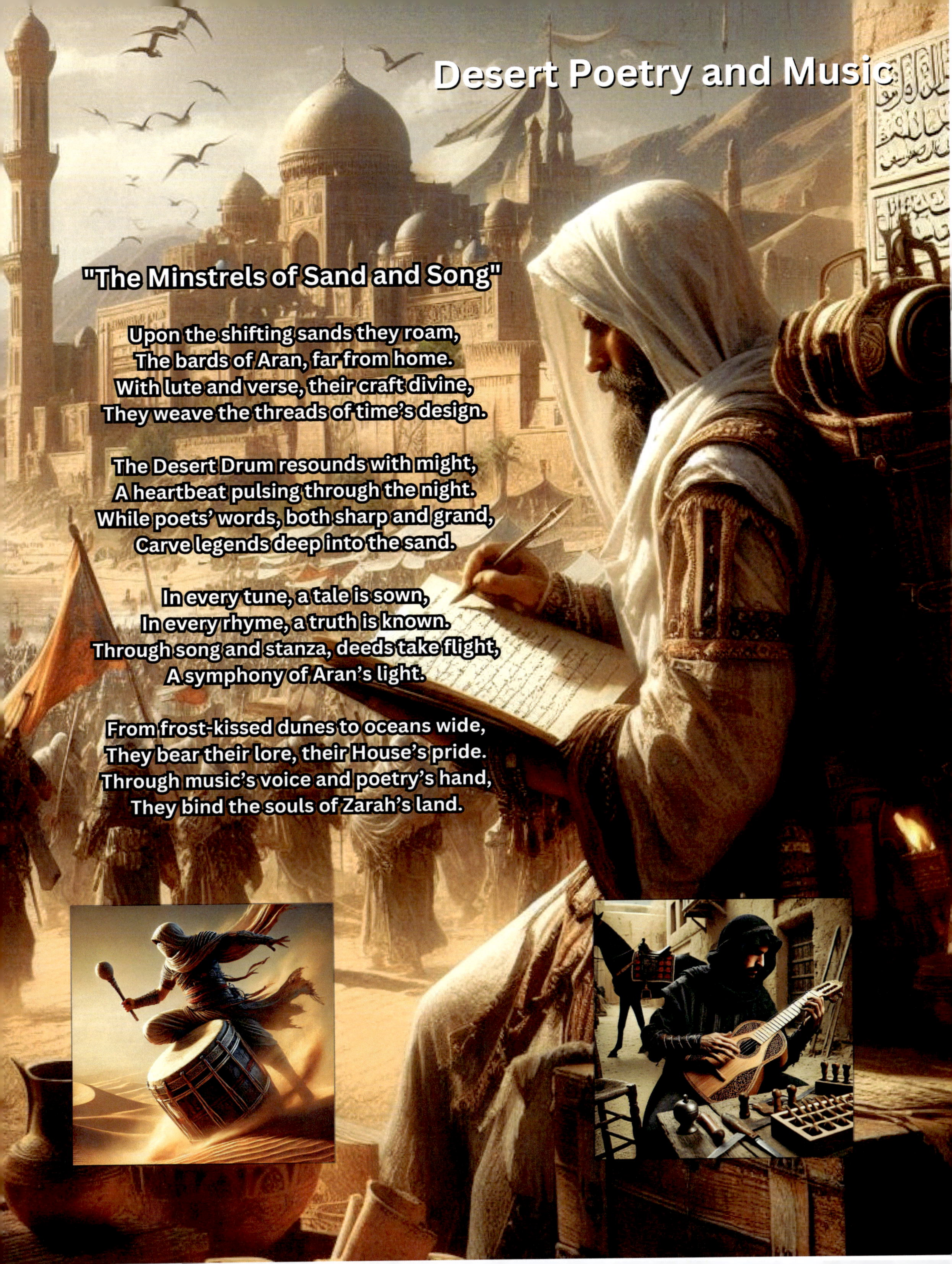

Desert Poetry and Music

"The Minstrels of Sand and Song"

Upon the shifting sands they roam,
The bards of Aran, far from home.
With lute and verse, their craft divine,
They weave the threads of time's design.

The Desert Drum resounds with might,
A heartbeat pulsing through the night.
While poets' words, both sharp and grand,
Carve legends deep into the sand.

In every tune, a tale is sown,
In every rhyme, a truth is known.
Through song and stanza, deeds take flight,
A symphony of Aran's light.

From frost-kissed dunes to oceans wide,
They bear their lore, their House's pride.
Through music's voice and poetry's hand,
They bind the souls of Zarah's land.

Cave Paintings and Rock Art

In the remote regions of Zarah, where the deserts give way to vast canyons and towering mesas, the Aran have left behind a remarkable legacy of cave paintings and rock art.

These ancient artworks, some dating back thousands of years, depict the lives and beliefs of the Aran's ancestors, offering glimpses into their worldview and their relationship with the land.

The cave paintings, often found in sheltered alcoves and hard-to-reach locations, feature vibrant depictions of desert wildlife, scenes of daily life, and symbolic representations of Aran spirituality.

The artists used natural pigments derived from the desert's minerals to create these works, blending them seamlessly with the rugged, textured surfaces of the rock.

Cave Paintings and Rock Art

Rock art, on the other hand, takes the form of intricate petroglyphs - carvings and etchings made directly into the stone.

These works showcase the Aran's mastery of stonework, as well as their deep connection to the physical landscape of Zarah.

From abstract geometric patterns to detailed renderings of horses, warriors, and celestial symbols, the rock art of the Aran stands as a testament to their enduring legacy and their unwavering bond with the desert realm.

Their art is not only a reflection of their environment but also a form of communication, used to pass down knowledge, tell stories, and solidify the identity of the Aran people.

Spirituality and The Priesthood of the Sun

Spirituality plays a vital role in the life of the Aran, with the desert itself seen as both a sacred and living entity.

The Priesthood of the Sun is the highest spiritual authority, responsible for interpreting the will of the stars and maintaining harmony between the people and the desert.

The priests believe that the desert speaks through the wind, the sun, and the shifting sands, and it is their duty to listen.

Ceremonies are held regularly to honour the desert, with offerings of water, food, and music made at specific sites, where the Ley lines of Zarah cross.

These rituals are vital for ensuring the continued prosperity of the Aran people, as it is believed that any disruption in the spiritual balance of the desert could lead to droughts, sandstorms, and famine.

The Priesthood of the Sun

"The Radiant Keepers"

In Zarah's expanse, where the sun's fierce flame,
Burns paths through sands that none can tame,
The Priesthood of the Sun holds sway,
Guiding Aran hearts through night and day.

Beneath the orbs' blazing gaze,
Their temples rise through desert haze.
Carved of stone where the ley lines meet,
They anchor faith where earth and sky greet.
Golden spires pierce azure heights,
Beacons of wisdom, eternal lights.

Clad in robes of solar hue,
The priests interpret the heavens' view.
With chants that stir the shifting air,
They weave the sands with cosmic prayer.
Each ritual, a sacred thread,
That binds the living to the dead.

Their voices summon the desert's grace,
To guard its people, to bless their space.
At dawn, they sing to the rising blaze,
At dusk, they whisper the twilight's praise.
Through them, the suns reveal their will,
Their truths inscribed in the desert still.

The Priesthood's hand shapes every art,
From lute's soft song to blade's swift dart.
Their teachings carve each poet's line,
And warriors fight with purpose divine.
Their wisdom flows through every vein,
A sacred balm for joy and pain.

When storms arise and shadows creep,
The priests stand firm where others weep.
With Solarwood staffs and hearts of flame,
They quell the chaos, their spirit untamed.
Their rites protect, their words inspire,
A bridge from fear to hearts' desire.

In every Aran's soul they dwell,
Their sacred lore, a guiding spell.
For through their light, the House is bound,
In desert's vast, where truths resound.

Oh Priesthood bright, oh keepers grand,
Your wisdom shapes this shifting land.
Through sands eternal, your flame shall burn,
A light to guide, a force to learn.

The Priesthood of the Sun
Guardians of the Aran Spiritual Realm

At the heart of the House of Aran's vibrant culture lies the Priesthood of the Sun, a revered order tasked with maintaining the sacred balance between the people and the desert realm of Zarah. These spiritual leaders are not merely tenders of rituals and rites, but interpreters of the desert's ancient wisdom, mediators between the physical and the metaphysical.

The Priesthood views the desert as a living, breathing entity, imbued with a sentience that transcends the physical. Through divination, meditation, and communion with the celestial bodies, the priests seek to decipher the will of the desert, translating its shifting sands, howling winds, and the dance of the sun into guidance for the Aran people. This deep, almost mystical connection to the land is the foundation of their authority and the wellspring of their sacred duty.

The Temple of the Sun in Shamaria stands as the spiritual epicenter of the Aran world, a place of profound reverence and power. Here, the High Priest and their council convene to perform the most sacred rituals, guiding the people through the cycles of the seasons and the turning of the celestial tides. It is said that the sands of the temple hold the memories of every Aran who has walked its halls, a living chronicle of the civilization's triumphs and trials.

Yet, the Priesthood's mandate extends beyond the purely spiritual. They are also the guardians of Aran society, charged with protecting the people from forces that would seek to unravel the delicate fabric of their way of life. Chief among these threats is the subversive influence of the House of Draco, a shape-shifting civilization known for its manipulative nature and hunger for power.

The Draco have long coveted the resources and strategic position of the Aran, and have made numerous attempts to infiltrate the Priesthood, seeking to sow discord and undermine the spiritual foundation of the Aran people. The priests, ever vigilant, have met these incursions with unwavering determination, using their divination skills and arcane knowledge to root out the Draco's agents and neutralize their machinations.

The Priesthood of the Sun
Guardians of the Aran Spiritual Realm

Awareness to the Draconian infiltration began to occur during the reign of High Priest Zahir, a century ago. Through a series of visions, Zahir detected a growing unrest within the ranks of the priesthood, a subtle shift in the desert's energies that hinted at Draconian interference. Assembling his most trusted disciplines, Zahir launched a covert investigation, tracing the source of the disturbance to a seemingly innocuous temple in the northern deserts.

What they uncovered was a complex web of deception, with Draco shapeshifters posing as Aran priests, subtly manipulating the rituals and sowing seeds of doubt among the faithful. The ensuing confrontation was a brutal one, as the Aran priests wielded their mastery of the desert's arcane forces to expose and expel the Draco infiltrators. The victory, while hard-won, solidified the Priesthood's reputation as stalwart defenders of Aran sovereignty and the sanctity of their civilization.

In the aftermath, the High Priest enacted sweeping reforms, strengthening the order's internal security protocols and establishing the Sacred Order, an elite cadre of priest-warriors tasked with safeguarding the Priesthood and the people against future Draconian incursions. This potent combination of spiritual wisdom and martial prowess has proven invaluable in the ongoing struggle against the shape-shifting machinations of the House of Draco.

Today, the Priesthood of the Sun stands as a beacon of stability and resilience in the Aran world, their influence and authority reaching into every corner of the six kingdoms. From the frigid northern deserts to the scorching southern sands, the priests are revered as both spiritual guides and protectors, their unwavering dedication to the desert's harmonious balance a testament to the enduring strength of the House of Aran.

As the sands of time continue to shift, the Priesthood remains vigilant, ever attuned to the subtlest fluctuations in the desert's energies, ready to confront any force that would dare to threaten the delicate equilibrium that sustains their civilization.
For in the Aran worldview, the desert is not merely a physical landscape, but a living, sacred realm that must be guarded with the utmost care and reverence - a sacred trust that the Priesthood of the Sun upholds with every fiber of their being.

99

The Order of the Sacred Desert
Guardians Against the Draconian Threat

Woven into the very fabric of Aran society is the Order of the Sacred Desert, an elite cadre of priest-warriors entrusted with the sacred duty of protecting the Priesthood of the Sun and safeguarding the spiritual integrity of the six kingdoms. Born from the crucible of the Draco's subversive machinations, this order stands as the bulwark against any force that would seek to undermine the delicate balance maintained by the desert's spiritual guardians.

The origins of the Order can be traced back to the reign of High Priest Zahir, who, in the wake of a Draconian infiltration of the Priesthood, recognized the need for a specialized force dedicated to rooting out such insidious threats. Drawing from the most adept warriors and most devout priests, Zahir handpicked the inaugural members of the Order, imbuing them with not only the martial prowess to confront the Draco's shape-shifting agents, but also the spiritual discernment to detect the subtlest of deceptions.

These priest-warriors are masters of the desert's arcane arts, their connection to the land's sacred energies granting them uncanny intuition and the ability to wield potent elemental magics. With their keen senses attuned to the ever-shifting sands, they can detect the faintest disturbances in the desert's ancient rhythms, a skill that has proven invaluable in rooting out Draconian infiltrators and neutralizing their subversive plots.

The Order of the Sacred Desert
Guardians Against the Draconian Threat

Another famed occurrence took place during the reign of High Priest Nasir, nearly a century after Zahir's reforms. Word reached the Order of a series of strange occurrences in the Coastal Deserts of Yara, where the local populace had reported unnatural phenomena – flickering lights in the night sky, whispers in the desert winds, and a growing sense of unease that permeated the very air. Dispatching a team of their most seasoned warriors, the Order launched a covert investigation, their senses attuned to the slightest hint of Draconian influence.

What they uncovered was a sinister plot to undermine the Yararians' trust in their spiritual leaders, with Draco shapeshifters posing as members of the local priesthood and subtly sowing seeds of doubt and discord among the people. Through a series of carefully orchestrated rituals and illusions, the Draco agents sought to erode the Yararians' faith in the Priesthood, hoping to create an opening for their own agents to infiltrate the corridors of power.

The Order of the Sacred Desert
Guardians Against the Draconian Threat

The ensuing confrontation between the Order and the Draco was a harrowing one, as the Order's priest-warriors engaged the Draconian infiltrators in a brutal display of martial prowess and arcane mastery. Wielding sacred blades forged from the rarest desert metals and imbued with the power of the elements, they battled the shape-shifting foes, their movements guided by the very sands beneath their feet. In the end, the Order emerged victorious, the Draconian plot thwarted and the Yararian priesthood cleansed of its corrupted members.

In the aftermath, the High Priest commended the Order's unwavering dedication and tactical brilliance, solidifying their reputation as the stalwart defenders of Aran spiritual sovereignty. The Order's success in Yara served as a stark warning to the House of Draco, making it clear that their subversive efforts would be met with the full force of the Aran's most elite and devoted protectors.

The Order of the Sacred Desert
Guardians Against the Draconian Threat

Today, the Order of the Sacred Desert remains ever-vigilant, their senses attuned to the subtle fluctuations in the desert's energy, ready to respond at a moment's notice to any threat that dares to challenge the Aran's way of life. From the frigid northern reaches to the scorching southern sands, their presence is a reassuring beacon, a testament to the Aran's resolute determination to safeguard the sacred balance of their civilization against all who would seek to disrupt it.

As the sands of time continue to shift, the Order of the Sacred Desert stands as an unyielding bulwark, their blades and their magic forged in the crucible of their devotion to the Aran people and the desert they call home. For in their unwavering commitment lies the very preservation of the Aran's spiritual legacy, a legacy that has endured for generations and will continue to stand strong against any force that dares to threaten its sanctity.

The Subversive influence of the House of Draco

The House of Draco, reptilians, known for their shapeshifting abilities and manipulative nature, have been a persistent thorn in the side of the House of Aran. Operating in the shadows, the Draco have made numerous attempts to infiltrate and undermine Aran society, seeking to exploit its vulnerabilities and disrupt the delicate balance that sustains their civilization.

The Draco's primary strategy has been to infiltrate the Priesthood of the Sun, the spiritual heart of Aran culture. Shapeshifting into trusted members of the priesthood, the Draco agents have wormed their way into positions of influence, subtly sowing seeds of doubt, discord, and heresy. They have sought to corrupt the rituals, reinterpret the sacred texts, and turn the priests against one another - all in an effort to weaken the spiritual foundation that binds the Aran people together.

The Subversive influence of the House of Draco

In addition to targeting the priesthood, the Draco have also sought to manipulate the power dynamics between the six kingdoms. They have instigated border disputes, encouraged economic rivalries, and even gone so far as to orchestrate small-scale conflicts between the kingdoms. The Draco's goal is to prevent the Aran from uniting against a common threat, keeping them divided and distracted.

The Aran, however, have not been entirely oblivious to these Draconian machinations. Over time, they have developed a keen awareness of the shape-shifters' tactics and have taken steps to counter their influence. The establishment of the Order of the Sacred Desert has been a critical move, as these elite guardians of the priesthood have dedicated their lives to ferreting out Draco infiltrators and preserving the sanctity of Aran spirituality.

The Subversive influence of the House of Draco

Wanting to ensure the safety of its peoples, the Aran have also invested heavily in intelligence gathering, employing a network of spies and informants to monitor the movements of the Draco and identify potential threats before they can take root. When evidence of Draconian involvement in a conflict or dispute arises, the Aran are swift to respond, dispatching their most skilled warriors and diplomats to neutralize the threat and restore order.

The Subversive influence of the House of Draco

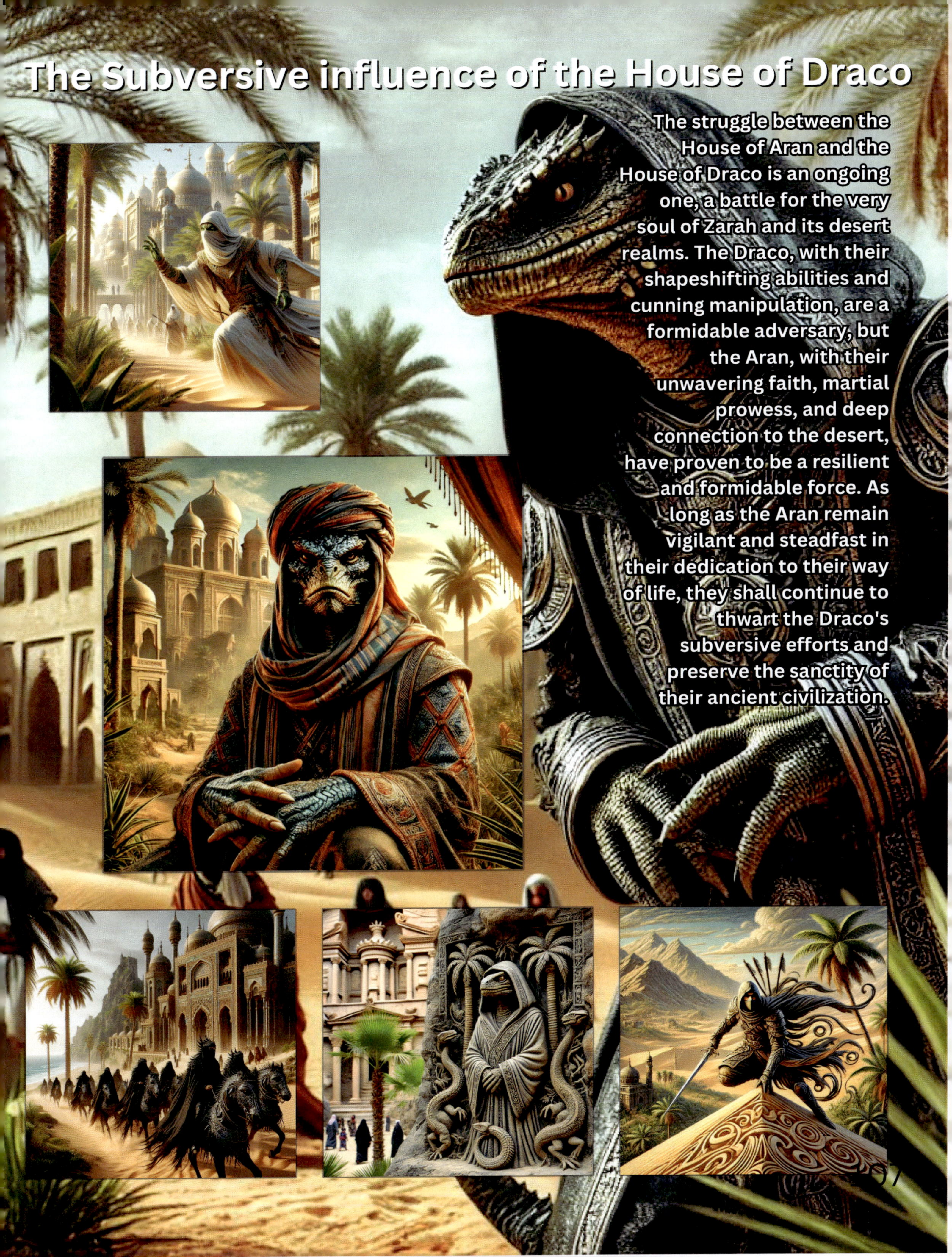

The struggle between the House of Aran and the House of Draco is an ongoing one, a battle for the very soul of Zarah and its desert realms. The Draco, with their shapeshifting abilities and cunning manipulation, are a formidable adversary, but the Aran, with their unwavering faith, martial prowess, and deep connection to the desert, have proven to be a resilient and formidable force. As long as the Aran remain vigilant and steadfast in their dedication to their way of life, they shall continue to thwart the Draco's subversive efforts and preserve the sanctity of their ancient civilization.

Guardians of the Desert Realms

The House of Aran, with its rich history, vibrant culture, and ongoing challenges, stands as a resilient and innovative civilization within the Leander System. Their achievements in adapting to the desert environment, their distinctive cultural practices, and their ongoing battles against, unbeknownst to them, external threats underscore their enduring strength and resourcefulness.

The Aran's commitment to preserving their way of life and defending their realms against subversive influences not only highlights their role as a significant, dynamic, and promising civilization but has also earned them the respect from the House of tempus. A House that lives outside the confines of physical reality, serving as observers, chroniclers, and keepers of time, and its flow, in The MiddleVerse.

Guardians of the Desert Realms

The Aran's ability to thwart the Draco's attempts at infiltration and subversion, through the vigilance of the Order of the Sacred Desert and their deep connection to the desert itself, is a testament to their resilience and adaptability. They have proven time and again that they are more than mere survivors - they are the guardians of the desert realms, imbued with a spirit that cannot be easily extinguished.

As the sands of Zarah shift and the celestial patterns evolve, the House of Aran remains steadfast in their duty to their homeland and their people. They stand as a beacon of hope in a universe that often favors the cunning and the ruthless, a civilization that has mastered the art of thriving in the most unforgiving of environments. The House of Aran stand as a testament to the enduring strength of the human spirit, a testament to the power of adaptation, and a reminder that even in the face of the most daunting challenges, Zarah's desert's children can rise to greatness.

THE HOUSE OF ARAN

Visual Guide